Dim White Phlox

A DECADE OF DISTANT CHILDHOOD
DERBYSHIRE

——————— 1937-1947 ———————

Terry Gilbert

© 1989

ISBN 0 946404 86 0

Printed and Published by
J. H. HALL & SONS LIMITED
Siddals Road, Derby
Printers and Stationers since 1831
Telephone: Derby (0332) 45218

THE DERBYSHIRE HERITAGE SERIES

To the people of the village of
Temple Normanton

PREFACE

I am often asked where I come from. People seize on my accent, curious to place it, and are invariably flummoxed when I tell them, proudly of course, that I hail from the North, from Derbyshire. "That's the Midlands", they scoff, "all that cloth cap stuff and D. H. Lawrence". Eastwood happens to be in Nottinghamshire, but they have got the cloth caps right, and if we are being pedantic and following the old rule of thumb about a line drawn level with the Wash, I suppose that 'Midlands' is technically correct.

There are, however, many other considerations of landscape, dialect, custom, lineage and affinities which help to establish my claim.

I was born in the Parish of Temple Normanton, (town of the Knights Templar) whose principal village was Bond's Main, (Mr. Bond's No. 1 shaft), a colliery village established towards the end of the last century, similar to many such places in Derbyshire's mining belt which runs like a scar across the county.

To the south lie great tracts of farmland, leading to the Dukeries and Sherwood Forest, and beyond, the real Midlands of Leicester, Birmingham, Warwick. To the north, in some places only a field away, never more than a couple of miles, and always visible on the horizon, is the edge of the moor. The Peak District climbs from there to valleys and dales, caverns, waterfalls and limestone crags, a landscape of overpowering beauty as different from the pastures and Downs of the South as a knife is to butter.

This heartland on the doorstep is the spiritual home of many an exile like myself. It was there that we roamed when I was a boy, in winds and weather straight from the Pennines. On high days and holidays we struck north, none of your Midlands for us, thank you.

At home, in the villages, there was a close knit life around the hearth, in compensation for the harsh exhausting work in the collieries. The original families had settled in the villages gratefully. They came from decaying moorland farms, the flats of Lincolnshire, Tyneside and Cumbria. Some of them were itinerants who had dug canals and railways and lived in rough shelters of boughs and sacking. They worked hard and struggled on small wages, but they had brand-new redbrick houses fitted with a sink, a Yorkshire range, and free coal to burn.

They forged the community into which I was born. Today it is gone. A motorway runs along the old embankment; the spoil tips, hundreds of thousands of tons, have been bulldozed away. The virgin land underneath them has been open-casted for yet more coal, then landscaped again into unlikely looking meadows, rising in artificial curves designed on a drawing board in a surveyor's office.

The rows of houses have vanished long ago, replaced by squat standardly acceptable bungalows such as you can find anywhere from Newhaven to Widnes, and the people I knew and loved are scattered, the old folks in Council Homes.

This book is an attempt to recall some of my early days. My memory has sometimes failed me, names are changed, separate incidents have blurred together, as have the characters, and I would find it difficult to say where fact merges with fiction.

Chapter I

SPRING AWAKENING

The boy, who was then just coming up to his fourth birthday lay still in the vast bed in the front room upstairs. The skivvy had been in, without saying a word, to wash him and comb his hair so that he should look alright for the doctor. Then she had straightened the sheets and mopped the lino floor before padding out, leaving the door ajar.

It was an all cream and white room swimming in a soft and blurry haze into which the milky sham-blind gazed down through the long morning, as the wind outside sent high clouds racing across the sky. The pale March sunlight filtered through the canvas, making a pair of eyes and a mouth in the cut-out loops and oversewn swirls of the pattern, while the curved fringe became the beard of a strange and comforting face which slowly emerged, draped by the shiny fawn curtains and glowing in the window like a saint on a Sunday School transfer.

Layers of flannel and blanket surrounded the boy. First the long grey shirt, and rag loose around his throat. Then the fine old christening shawl wound around his still body, the fluffed up pillows next, a thick eiderdown, warm as a breast and last the cool, smooth white counterpane.

He lay with his head on one side, the cotton cold to his cheek, looking at the picture on the wall of a farmhouse surrounded by blue trees, frozen with moonlight into the gilt frame. Then he slowly turned his head to the other side, taking in the dusty landscape of the ceiling. His stare followed a long crack in the plaster, a great fissure between rocks, thick swirls of whitewashed snowstorm sky piled with clouds and a sea full of towering waves which spilled over the moulding and the picture rail on to the green cord holding up the same farm and trees, rusty and warm in the autumn colours version. Below that was the never-used painted firegrate stuffed with yellow newspaper shaped into a fan.

On the mantelpiece the pale blue girl and the pale green boy turned towards each other, never speaking. They must have said something once, he thought, as their lips were open and almost smiling, but he felt guilty if the scarlet was faded because he had sometimes stolen in to kiss them. Every time he had put them each back carefully in the rings in the dust, but the faint chink of the figures on the iron shelf had echoed round the stairway down into the shop, and joined the voices droning on below like bees. The bees came buzzing up through the open door to settle on the palm-leaves of the wallpaper, two brown leaves curling upwards, one large green, three yellow, a thick branch, a stripe, then start again, and he fell once more into a deep cocooned sleep.

It was early afternoon, with the men and children all away from the houses. Mam leaning on the counter, and the women standing arms folded over pinafores, chins lowered into dark voices moving over the secret ground of fireguard talk. It would be dark in the shop long before tea-time, the gas mantle lit and the shutters closed. When the boy was older, he sometimes was caught in the passageway, a stranger at the ritual, his heart beating like a sparrow in the hand, desperate to listen and running the risk of understanding, but not hearing anything properly for the great pounding in his temples. But this was the first time the child recognized the conspiracy in the talk, and it had a strange comfort.

It was a long illness. The parents went very quietly and sat silent in the kitchen a long time after the old doctor's visits. They were getting no assurance, but they had to deal with plenty of hot poultices, wet flannels and vomit, and they felt much better when they were occupied than during the boy's endless sleeping in between.

Some of the women went upstairs without asking, to sit for a while in the wicker chair, watching out for a sign of brighter life. When the men came in, they were on their best behaviour and took their caps off, as they paid for a lump of twist or a tin of tobacco. If they asked how the lad was, missus, Mam would rub her hands together, worn smooth from rubbing her apron to ease the odd pain in her throat, thank them kindly and say she would have to wait and see. But one day the dreaming was over. Matt stumbled out of bed and called down the stairs, "Dad, dad, mam, can yer come? What am I in your bed for?"

Mrs. Bedford finished serving somebody a quarter of potted meat before she went up. She drew in a sharp breath and watched the greaseproof paper quiver between her fingers.

"Eh, missus, that's your lad shoutin', e's gor outta bed," said Mrs. Bates.

The needle on the weighing scale went over and hovered. Mam had thought she'd never hear him call again.

"Tek anythin' else yer want an' pay me tomorrow, Gladys, ah'd better go up. Nah, is there owt else for thee, Ma Lawton?"

"Nay, ah doan't want owt else while that lad's up theer maundering, lass. Ah'll come up wi' thee."

The two of them went upstairs, but Ma Lawton went in first while Mam got her breath back.

"Eh, lad, what thar doing out o' bed? Let's get thee back and keep thissen warm. Thar not reight yet, thar knows. Oah, Missus, it's gunna tek a long time, but that's a good sign, 'im gettin' up 'issen, ah reckon. Ah'd gi'e 'im some milk pobs in a bit if ah were thee. Eeh, thi mam's bin that wurried, she' bin that upset, tha little bugger. 'As thar gorra kiss for me? Anyway, ah think tha's growed, mi little sargeant-major. We'll 'ave thee in t'band yet we shall."

Mrs. Bedford waited till Mrs. Lawton had gone home to get her men their tea. Then she hurried to put the bolt on the shop door, and ran down to the railway in her slippers to call Dad.

"Eh, Jack, where's our lad? Tell 'im ah want 'im. Young un's got up. Ah'll 'ave to nip back. Tell 'im ter 'urry. Theer's nob'dy wie 'im. Eeh ah'm that chuffed."

As she ran back up the hill the voices rang out behind her down the line.

"Jess Bedford, eh, Jess Bedford. Get off 'ome. Thi missus wants thee. Lad's alreight, gerra move on. Ar lad's rabbit's just had some young uns. Would he like one?"

"Ah'll gie thee bloody rabbit. We doan't want no rabbits. Well, did she say our Matt's alreaight then? Ah'd better be off and 'ave a look at 'im."

Jess left his pick and shovel on the cutting, deep in the primroses, plucked a sprig of the heady white yarrow for the peak of his cap, and ran off up the back yards to the coal-house. He banked the fire in the back kitchen to a blaze, set up the clothes horse, draped with damp sheets for a hot-box, and gently carried Matt in like a sick colt to be coddled better.

"Thee stop theer, young whiskers, an' ah'll see thee better soon. Thar needs some warmth in thi back, and thar need some rubbin' wi' olive oil. We'll 'ave to feed thee up, mi owd flower, shan't we? An' thar wain't be goin' out yet for a while, it's bloody perishin' out theer. See mi knuckles, chapped and cut lousy wi' t'frost, thar not shiftin' from 'ere till ah've got thee in proper fettle."

Every day Dad came home for his dinner instead of taking his snap with him, and at four o'clock, when the pit shut and the traffic on the line eased off, he ran home to make toast in front of the fire for Matt. He sang a lot as he busied himself around the kitchen, while Mam joked herself back into the routine of the shop.

Chapter II

MARCH AIR

A few days later, in two vests, two jerseys, an overcoat and beret, Matt was put out for the air. His mother wrapped him in a striped knitted scarf which she crossed over at the front and tied in a knot at the back.

"Tha'll be real chuff in that, ma duck. Get thissen some o' them cobwebs blown off."

A kiss, a stick of liquorice, a clean hankie, off into the bitter March wind, with his eyes swimming, into a sea of air. The high white clouds flounced through the thick blue sky and shouted out to Matt that he was alive. He stood in the wind listening to the awesome jangle of the pit at full tilt mid-morning till the rawness blew him like a scrap of paper across the field. The telephone wires overhead sang out to a few squawking crows and passing seagulls which fell squealing down to the cobbled path between him and the row of houses nearby. Suddenly in front, there was Rose Lakinshawe, akimbo in apron and lisle stockings. She was as tall and straight as a clothes prop as she stood throwing bread to the birds.

When she saw Matt across the waste ground she let out a hoarse shriek, throwing her scrawny arms out wide. Her steel-rimmed glasses flashed under her iron grey permanent waves. Body bent forward, bright eyes piercing like a hungry wading bird, her legs brought her running forward, a giant on stilts. She pounced on him.

"Oh, it's thee, is it? Ah thowt tha'd never come ovver. A've bin watchin' thee. Thar looks proper poorly ter me, real lost, ma luvvly. Our Monica's just got up. She's bin badly as well. Ah doan't know, that mun a bin kissin' 'er again. It's catchin'. Come on lad, yer can both look at 'er new Rupert book what she 'ad for Christmas."

Monica was perched in the corner of the big leather settle, thin, tear stained and sniffing. A twist of tissue paper holding an ounce of sherbert might have had more weight and colour. The Rupert Annual lay open across the flank of the huge greyhound which stretched the length of the sofa, open jawed and dribbling over the edge.

Matt climbed over the dog and found himself a nest in the pile of old newspapers and comics next to Monica. Rose pounded at the washtub in the corner of the kitchen, half visible through the steam rising from the sheets and towels drying on the fireguard, while the dog lay panting, great moist tongue outstretched; and Rupert and a curious Chinese wizard went on a long mysterious journey, spelt out laboriously by Monica between sniffs and blowings into her rag.

With an enormous extra spurt of energy Mrs. Lakinshawe attacked the table in the middle of the room. She swept everything off on to the sideboard, splashed half a lading can of blue water from the tub and attacked with brushes until the wood oozed damp with starch and Dolly Dye.

"Get yer dinners then," she yelled, giving a final wild wipe with a cloth.

The children stood to the table, scorching the backs of their legs at the fire. There was an oven tin that had held the pork roast a few days before. The meat had gone, but they delved into the dark layer of stuffing embedded in jelly, and rubbed crusts of new bread into the fat with their fingers, thinking they were lucky if they found a bit of crackling.

"That'll put some 'airs on yer chest, young Matt, wain't it," said Rose, laughing between gulps of hot tea. She was leaning on one elbow by the copper, idly holding the curtain to one side, looking out at the day. Through the circle she had cleared on the steamed-up window with the end of her cardigan sleeve, she could see a young girl out on the field calling in all directions. The figure moved nearer Mrs. Lakinshawe's house.

"It's your Ev, out lookin' for thee ah should think. Better finish up and get goin'. Ah'll just go to 'er an' let 'er know tha'r 'ere."

Rose unlatched the door a few inches, calling out, "Come 'ere lass if ther lookin' for t'Bedford's lad. E's 'ere wi' our Monica." Evelyn ran across from the middens and stood just off the whitened step.

"Eeh, 'is Mam's bin that aflamed wi worry. Ah told 'er 'e couldn't 'a' gone far, but she's got everybody out lookin'. She knows he wain't 'ave got lost but she's all mithered about 'im 'avin' bin poorly, she'll be all of a muck sweat 'erself if she doan't look aht. Well thank yer Mrs. Lakinshawe. Ah'd best tek 'im 'ome nah. Say cheerio then."

She took hold of Matt's collar and led him back across the field.

The shop glowed a sulphurous yellow as the afternoon was closing, and inside the gas fire hissed a warm flame. Mrs. Bedford reached inside one of the glass jars for a twisted barley sugar coated in frost when she saw the girl bringing her lad down the path. Matt squirmed his way round the carpet-slippered women and their baskets, and crept under the counter flap, sliding his back very slowly along the familiar dark brown varnish paper. His mother picked him up by the thick folds of his scarf, slinging him over her shoulder so that his knees dug deep into her bosom. Her left hand sidled round her back, gently teasing with the barley stick. She stood swaying for some time while Matt sucked the sweet, listening to Evelyn sing in the kitchen as she ran fresh water into the kettle.

Evelyn was sixteen then and had been the Bedford's girl since she left school. She did the paper rounds every morning, evening and Sundays, cleaned out the house and shop, swilled the yard, made the tea, polished, scrubbed and fettled all day. Friday was blackleading day, as in all the other houses of the village. The fire range had to be dismantled, flues raked, brass polished, oven scraped, the hearth scoured, and then all be re-assembled for the master to come home to a bright fire.

Evelyn made light of the work, crooning in a high thin monotone as she blackleaded and rubbed till her knuckles were the same colour as the hob. After that, the cutlery drawer was emptied, fettled out and re-lined with fresh wax paper. Every knife, fork and spoon, even the tin openers, sharpening steel, tea strainers and rolling pin were tackled with a variety of strong smelling fluids and powders.

Mam Bedford would come out of the shop for a minute, run a finger along the window sill and say, "You're a good lass, Ev, there's only them winders to do now, then thar can go 'ome to thi' mam."

Matt often stood out in the back yard hardly daring to move about the swilled, gleaming blue bricks for fear of Evelyn's wrath after she had given them such a good going over. He watched the bird-like girl climb about the outside window, rubbing the panes with a squeaky chamois, blowing harsh little bursts of breath, till he feared the glass would explode. Then while Matt stood whistling she would, with marvellous precision, draw her own patterns on the sills and doorstep, filling them in with rubstone so that the house could be declared fit for the weekend.

That late afternoon, while Evelyn cut the bread in the kitchen the shop went quiet while Mam gave Matt five minutes, as she called it. Then the women, who had been leaning on their elbows, or standing with their hands on their hips, purse-lipped and smiling, took him over for a while and passed him from one to another, clucking about his peaky looks, his thin body and his lustreless eyes, with a great deal of advice about chicken fat, yeast, raw eggs, and some beastings from the farm if they happened to have a cow in calf.

"Ay, there's nowt worse than a sickly kid," said Ma Lawton.

"You're right, duck," Mrs. Bates broke in rather sharply, anxious to tell how terrible it had been when her Laura had got bad with the mumps and then Derek had his tonsils out down at the General.

But Mrs. Bedford knew that her favourite story was the more compelling, and that her customers would give her their rapt attention again as if they were hearing it for the first time. So she quickly interrupted by reaching over to take the child back from Mrs. Barlow.

"Well, ah'll just weigh you that half pound o' cheese, Nell, did you want the Cheddar or American Red? Ah'll put 'im down 'ere on t'floor, 'e can play in that bottom drawer wi' marbles and t'whippin' tops."

She moved a tray of custard tarts away to the side to make room for the cheese wire and board, and as she took hold of the cutters in her thick capable hands, her heavy breasts rose beneath her apron.

"There were a time, ah can tell yer, ah'd 'ave rather done without, Enid Bates, if yer want ter 'ear of my worst trouble ever I 'ad. There's times sometimes when ah think we're just sent on ter this earth to suffer, and ah've 'ad more than my share, ah'll 'ave yer know. This little bugger, 'e nearly killed me when 'e come into this world. There's not many 'as could go through what ah've bin through and do the work ah've done and come through it wi'out grumblin'. I 'ad my share, and my belly aches still ter think about it, and if it 'adn't bin for our Jess, eh 'e were a good lad that day, ah wouldn't be ere ter tell t'story."

She bent down to open a drawer of cotton reels for Matt to play with, ruffling his hair and squeezing the back of his neck, while the women settled themselves appreciatively along the counter-top. When she rose she faced the group for a long moment, relishing the intimacy of their attention.

"Jess were on t' early shift, ah remember, and he said 'ow 'e'd try and get 'ome straight after dinner time 'cos 'e knew ah was due. Bloody 'ell though, about twelve o'clock I 'ad this terrible feelin' come over me. It seared right through me, like ah thought ah were on fire. Ah started ter bleed and ah tried to get upstairs but all ah could do was get as far as t'bottom step and ah collapsed. Them stairs is very steep yer know, and no 'andrail or bannister, and ah remember just lying there looking up and thinkin' it were like a mountain I 'ad ter get up. Well, ah crawled up on mi' 'ands and knees, and then our Jess's dog come rushin' up 'owlin' and scrabblin', tryin' ter lick me. 'E were all ovver me, and 'e were a bloody great slavverin' thing. Bull dog 'e was, and 'e 'ad great pink eyes an' a pug nose. Well, God knows 'ow ah did it, but ah got to t'top and ah'd half got into t'bed when its head came out an' then all that bag 'e were in. I could 'ave died. Ah screamed and choked but there were nobody come. T'dog were goin' mad. 'E'd rush up barkin' and snarlin' and then jump up on t'bed 'howlin' like a very devil. Thank God Jess got back. 'E run upstairs and kicked that dog from t'top ter bottom. When 'e come in, t'dog t'were tryin' to get to t'cord between me and t'babby. He picked up t'babby and put it on t'bed next ter me, then 'e threw t'winder up and shouted for somebody to fetch old Mrs. Raybould. She ran round and managed me and t'lad alreight. But that were a funny comin' into t'world for this babby o'mine weren't it?" Mrs. Bedford seized the boy into her arms, smothering his face with her kisses.

"Ay, but it were worth it for a bit o'fluff and cuddle like thee though, bless thi cotton socks, an' ah hopes thar never 'as ter go through what thi poor old mam 'as 'ad to."

There was a long pause while the women reflected on their lot before they gathered up their purchases and drifted home to wait the men off the afternoon shift.

Evelyn came briskly down the passage to fetch Matt for his tea which was laid out neatly on the kitchen table, while Mrs. Bedford wandered down the front path to the gate.

Orange streaks of light were flickering from the horizon beyond the wood framing the valley, and the wheel of the pit cage turned in a black vortex through the smoke which rose from the tall chimney, spiralling higher than the sunset.

She shivered as the wind blew along the lane, rustling the lattice fence and the dried up privet flowers which hung in brown clusters on the hedge. The gantry, which led over the railway line up into the blackened corrugated dome of the shaft housing, creaked noisily as the first men shuffled home. At that moment her heart felt as hard and grey as the hill of slag which towered over the marshalling yard, and she wanted to cry out in answer to the sheets of metallic noise which filled the dusty air.

Chapter III

THE NEW ADMISSION

After a few more weeks, when he had completely recovered from the illness, Matt was sent to join the nursery class conducted by Grannie Horsmann in the village school. Evelyn led him by the hand across the cinder track but he darted into her mother's house nearby when he saw the riot of children assembling outside the big green gates. Mr. Drew lifted him up into the stone sink underneath the window and pulled aside the stained lace curtain.

"Thar'd better 'urry up, young un'," he growled, tweaking Matt's ear, "and get thissen over theer by t'time yon old crow dingles 'er bell, or thar'll be in trouble no mistake, even if it is thi first day. By, she's an old tartar, ah know 'cos she were theer when ah were a lad. She must be bloody eighty if she's a day. Thar doesn't want to cross 'er on t'first day, nah, does thar?"

"Leave off Ted, leave 'im be," called Mrs. Drew, bent over the range with oven cloths, turning her baking tins. "Ah'll walk 'im in when I've put these loaves in for 'is mam."

Crossing over to Matt, she gently lifted him down, smoothed his hair and wiped his tear-stained face with a soapy flannel.

"Nah then, duck, if thar a good lad and comes wi' me wi' no bother, ah'll get our Jack to show thee 'is ferrets when 'e comes 'ome this afternoon from t'pit. Come 'ere when t'bell goes at four o'clock. E'll be 'ome by then and you can 'elp 'im to feed 'em. But only if thar behaves thissen."

On the clang of the bell they went together along the flagstone path which led past the middens and the chicken pen towards the school gate. By this time Granny Horsmann was cajoling the children into two separate lines of boys and girls. As they jostled dutifully into place, she clucked and prodded them with her cane. To Matt she appeared an awesome figure, dressed all over in black, her bombazine blouse studded in jet, and her long skirt falling over buttoned boots. The wispy grey waves were pulled back untidily into a bun on the nape of her wrinkled neck, and an alarming wart on her chin sprouted a fierce tuft of hair which jabbed up and down in the air as she marched the children around the school yard. Catching sight of Matt, she bellowed at the lines to come to attention and came forward briskly to inspect the new entrant. Matt seized hold of Mrs. Drew's sacking apron and tried to hide behind it, but the teacher prodded him with her stick and without a word bustled him through the cloakroom into the hall.

"Sit down here right in front of me, Matt Bedford, and wipe your nose.

If you haven't got a handkerchief, remember to bring one this afternoon. I don't like little boys who wipe their noses on their jerseys, a terrible habit to be avoided if you please. Rise children," she commanded. "Hands together, eyes closed, let us say our morning prayer together. Our Father," began Granny Horsmann, and in a monotone the class followed.

Matt had done as bid, but his eyes opened wide at the idea of his father being in heaven and the strangeness of them all asking his own dad for their bread every day. After the spoken part of the ceremony the mistress produced a tuning fork from her embroidered vanity case and led the class lustily through 'All Things Bright and Beautiful'. During the singing Matt shifted his feet uneasily and stole a few glances around the room. The ochre walls resounding to the hymn were covered in waxed prints of the flowers, fruit, birds and butterflies to which the hymn seemed to refer, and a haloed Jesus stood framed in a field of lilies over which spread a pastel coloured rainbow.

Granny Horsmann waved her arms energetically, keeping the piping voices together, her own voice underlining them in a deep contralto, while the knife-edged pleats of her blouse rose and fell in time with the singing. In her enthusiasm, wild strands of her untidy coiffure detached themselves and with one hand she vainly attempted to push them back behind her ears. Her reddened, veined cheeks glistened with the effort but she continued to sing lustily to the end of the hymn, and dabbing at her face with a lace handerchief she recovered her composure while the pupils clattered down into their chairs.

They tittered amongst themselves as they got out their slates and chalks for the lesson which was already prepared on the easel at the front of the class, but at one rap of the cane on the desk an impressive silence fell in the vaulted room. The bewildered Matt froze at his desk, his feet twisted around the legs of his chair, and his thumbs pushed tightly into the tops of his socks for comfort.

Faintly at first, and gradually rising in a great murmuring crescendo, there came through the dividing glass partition the sound of an older adjacent class reciting their tables. Counting and spelling exercises reverberated in a plaintive chant which echoed in the arches overhead, numbing Matt's ears to the work proceeding in his own classroom. In the distance doors banged and desk-lids clattered, authoritative voices barked sharp interruptions, and occasionally steam-trains thundered past in the cutting, rattling the vast window. Meanwhile the pupils shuffled their feet relentlessly on the tiled floors, the coloured beads shunted across the wire counting frames and Granny Horsmann tapped her cane along the rows of desks.

As the morning wore on, the anthracite stove in the corner crackled out its pungent heat, causing a musky stench to rise from the young bodies enmeshed in corduroy and moleskin. The perspiring dame erased the

characters on the blackboard, causing a fine talc to float in the hot air from
her brisk application of the felt rubber and then began again patiently with
squeaking chalks, pausing sometimes to lick the dust from her fingers.
Suddenly outside a monitor rang the bell for a break and the children
dutifully filed outside.

Out in the yard the children raced and tumbled in great heaps on the
hard tarmac. Holding their noses against the stench of carbolic they rushed
in and out of the lavatories, daring boys jostling open doors in the girls
cubicles, grabbing knickers and pulling stockings down. When they saw a
great spurt of smoke and steam in the distance down the line they
scrambled up the wall and sat astride the parapet, cheering the
approaching goods train, shrieking to the guard who waved his flag back at
them.

The bell rang again and Mrs. Horsmann appeared at the door to lead
them back in to labour for the remainder of the morning.

In the dinner hour the children who lived nearby were allowed home,
but those from outlying parts stayed behind eating bread and dripping in
the garden shed. Evelyn came to the gate, sent by Mrs. Bedford to fetch
Matt home. They were delighted to see the boy race through his dinner so
that he could get back to the games in the yard. They played whips and
tops, dobbers, hopscotch and alarum, and the girls whooped around with
skipping rhymes until the bell.

That afternoon, and for the rest of his time in the dame's care, Matt was
nurtured in the course of the seasons and the simple basics of learning.

Beans sprouted in jam jars between the glass and damp blotting paper,
next to saucers of bitter cress and hot mustard. The boys threaded conkers
by number while the girls learned to stitch their names in thick red wool on
cardboard. From nature walks they brought back bunches of coltsfoot or
bluebells and counted them out laboriously into vases where they wilted
and died on the shelves above the hot radiators.

The old lady's maxim was simple. Her children must be courteous, learn
their numbers, read, write and spell before they left her charge. She hailed
from Derby, born to a middle class family of doctors and clergymen settled
comfortably in some sophistication in a large red-brick manse, well
provided and ordered.

Since she had arrived in this upland, raw village, she had seen much
poverty and neglect, even cruelty. Most of her children were poorly
dressed, sometimes barefoot and undernourished. They were destined to
become farmworkers, miners and skivvies, and she had determined to
instil in them some common-sense, a fear of God, the elements of
personal hygiene, good health and basic literacy. These were qualities and
requirements to sustain them later on through their hard labouring lives
with extra mouths to feed.

The rigours experienced by her old scholars caused her much pain, especially the suffering of the men who were injured in the pits. Boys left her school at fourteen to toil in the shale as apprentice colliers. They aged prematurely when they began on the underground seam, their faces disfigured by deep blue scars and their bodies stooped from the cold and damp.

The unlucky ones lost a leg or some of their fingers when heavy tubs of coal ran away down ramps, colliding and crushing them. Or a man could die pinned under tons of rock, choked in foul poisoned air. At worse, he could survive and live his life out on a couch in a front parlour.

When terrible accidents occurred, Granny Horsmann offered counsel and practical advice. If others helped with food and clothing in a way that she could not manage on her small annual stipend, she had vowed, she would use her trained mind to see that proper applications were made for compensation, medical treatment and injury benefits. She waged a holy war with pit managers and deputies and wept when one of her young boys died in the seam.

The villagers were grateful for her help when they needed it. They doffed their caps and accorded to her their due respect, but she remained a foreigner in their midst, still resented for her polished vowels and fastidious manners.

A lad might get up from the bench outside the public house and take his beer inside if he saw her walking up the lane, and the old men would lower their heads in staring silence, but the old lady would pass by erect and smiling on her way to the four o'clock bus.

Chapter IV

THE START OF MAY

Mrs Barlow eased her large frame away from the back door jamb where she had been watching the day, and ambled over the waste ground on the other side of the bottom road. She clucked at a couple of hens from Bob Sewell's pen on her way over the fence. It was a late autumn afternoon. The air down the railway embankment was hot and heavy, like her forearms and breasts hanging resting on the polished toprail. She moved her wide hips over to one side and scratched the back of one leg with the other foot in its dusty gym shoe, lost in a kind of love with the aching familiarity of everything ahead of her. Long brown grass tussocked and mangled, the docks gone to seed, orange and yellow toadflax and wild antirhinums standing erect amid the drooping scabious; like the patterns of a well worn hall carpet leading into a room, they led her eye down over the shining steel rails and glittering cobbled track to the yards. She focussed on the baking ovens in the middle of the yard, and fell into a drowse with the red glow coming through the open doors. A man came up the ramp pushing a barrow of clay. Another man came out of the finishing shed on the right with a load of new bricks on a trolley, warm and burnt like fresh loaves. The afternoon sun still beat hot and there was a gold varnish spread thick over the purple brick of the kilns, the dust caught spangled and unmoving, Mrs. Barlow held her breath, and stretched her back for a long moment, till with a deep sigh she folded her arms again and fell in wonder at the magic of this and endless other afternoons.

She began humming to herself, some strange tune she had never heard before, her head moving side to side, with her chin feeling the backs of her hands. After a while she started to tap the polished top rail of the fence with her thick worn wedding ring to the same rhythm, but she got out of time and caught her breath sharply when she saw her husband open the door of the drying chamber at the top of the opposite bank and step blinking into the light. Twisting her ring round and round her finger she thought about her eight children, the seven never-ending boys and then the last unexpected little girl. That was a blessing. Funny how they had all been fair and then this last shiny black haired thing. Like a water rat when it was born, she had thought, with that long black hair lying wet and flat stuck to her neck. Squashed up thick eyelids and bulges all over her face she had, just like a little animal, and how long it took for her eyes to open. But when it was a bit older, what a joy this child had been though. It had livened up their all male household, changed things a lot, even though she never much thought of it one day turning into another woman like herself. And grand to have a different set of little clothes hanging on the brass rail drying over the fire. She had lain a long time with this last baby, feeling wasted in a great heap of exhaustion, wondering how she would ever live through another one. The weight and wear of those heavy lads had worn her down, and it was so peaceful for once to let them get on without her. After all she had earned a rest.

Better have it out with Frank when he comes in this afternoon she had thought. He's that shy, talking about these things. Won't even talk at the time. Even now he still rolls over pretending to be asleep before he starts. He's that funny in the morning turning his back, fumbling with his shirt flap, hiding it like he's not got one. It's all very well, but he doesn't have to pay the price. His own mother died having her tenth. He can't be pretending he's forgotten that one. Next time he turns over and puts his hand on my belly I shall ask him if it's another kid he wants, and though he's a good man who'd never wish us any harm, and he works hard and brings home every penny, and he doesn't get with the others drinking all and every night, he's got to think on and realise I'm not as young as I was. He's got to start thinking more about me. These kids don't want an old mother, and he'd be no good without me. It's alright now while the fun lasts. Listen, just listen to him down there singing at the top of his voice coming through the gennil. The kettle's on the hob. He'll get the boys' tea and then he'll scrub them up in the sink. He'll send me a cup of tea up, but he won't come up unless there's something he can't find.

She had fondled the baby and squirmed in her tiredness. The baby lay on her own body, rising up and down like a little boat on a wave. She pressed its head deep into the fat of her belly and, grasping the little hand pushed it around trying to show it where it had come from. Later the baby lay across the top of her thighs after she had fed and changed it. She prised open the fat, tight fist and kissed the sweet smelling palm. Madge Barlow, she thought, what are you going to call this little thing? Frank's mother was called May, and it must be thirty years almost since she died. Would he like her to be called after her? This one wouldn't die though, she'd see to that. Not this little darling. She fell into a half sleep sitting there stooped forward. Her jaw hung slack and her cheeks pouched away from her teeth, till the space inside her mouth felt huge and still. A thought formed in the black hollow there and passed up the dark breathing to her tired brain, as dimly coloured and unclear in its pattern as the lino fading like a mist before her half closed eyes. It started numbly like a pain but it cleared as she fell back in slow motion on to the pillows. When her head was still she closed her eyes tightly listening to the sparrows and boys outside. An enormous wave of light came rolling into her daydreams, cascading over the fields into the allotments, and broke up into fingers poking through between the stoops at the bottom of the yard. The sheets on next door's line billowed like a huge white sail, and a feeling of contentment rolled over the top of the open window. Great crests of clouds moved on past the distant tip mountains, brushing the single elm tree close by the old Hall at Scarsdale. There was a gymkhana and picnic over there once, deep in her memory, the brassy music and the rippling waters of the lake trying to ebb towards her. A cloud shaped like a canoe stopped and hovered over the sheets which now hung limp and dry outside. She rolled her tongue around her mouth and wondered if the tea would come. The canoe moved on through the blue water. She could just make out the shape of a young man bending over May who was lying back in her cream shantung. As he took her hand in his, she pressed the baby's fist close to her, but the pleasure soon went out of it, and she rolled the small bundle over and listened intently to its breathing. The pictures in her mind faded and she begun to breathe in time with the child, in the same sharp hissing way, until the cloud passed the window.

The flames of the ovens across the cutting curled in the afternoon sun. Frank pushed a barrow down the slope and turned the corner towards the time-shop where he would clock off for the day. A sudden bell, the school doors opening, and the shrill sounds of the children screaming out of the yard. The four o'clock slow train for Derby came round the bend, sending up a long trailing curve of grey smoke. The engine driver waved, but she was already turning to go back across the waste ground to put the kettle on and get the tea.

Chapter V

COVERT LOVE

Old Man Drew, with Matt on his knee, sat rocking in the kitchen. He playfully rubbed his stubbly chin on the boy's soft cheek, wheezed, occasionally poked the fire and spat in the grate.

"Let's be off up yon timber then," he said, reaching for his knobbed stick and his cap.

They gathered up the other children, including May, who had been squatting on the doorstep, munching lumps of turnip handed over by Ma Drew who was chopping up a stew.

The group meandered down the lane towards the wood. The old man thrashed the nettles down with his stick and poked about the hedgerows looking for nests. He came across a wood pidgeon brooding in a hawthorn. The bird's eyes flickered momentarily, then settled into a terrified glazed stare until the stick was suddenly thrust into the bush and away she went flapping and screeching. Drew lunged at the little platform of twigs till the eggs were smashed and the bright yellow yolks dripped through and fell in streams on the turf underneath.

Overhead trilling larks hovered and darted, sometimes climbing so high they were like specks of dust, and the children held their hands up around their eyes, squinting into the sunlight.

They wandered on gathering buttercups till they came to a wooden bridge over a stream from where they threw stones at a pair of moorhens. Further up the bank some boys had dammed the water on a wide bend and were swimming naked in the brackish water. There was a sluice gate to dive from and a narrow culvert through which the boys rode on logs, splashing around in the livid green algae. Their bodies were curiously pale and thin against the lush undergrowth of the banks. When they saw Old Man Drew and the children, the boys darted into the water like rats, and hid in the reeds. May called out brazenly, "Bare buff, bare buff, come on lads, show us yer bare buff."

Over the bridge they stepped quietly into the wood through a deep litter of leaves crumbling into decay. Their feet sank pleasantly in the moist compost and trampled clumps of celandines. The faint breeze stirred the wild anemones into action so that they trembled from white to pink, and straggling water cress swayed in the brook.

Further on, the ground became more spongy, the moss spiked with bullrushes and willow herb. A robin flew low from a hole in a tree trunk.

Matt was fearful that Drew had seen the flash of red, but the sharp eyed old man was seeking out caterpillars on the angelica and grinding them with his boot.

The barely discernible path led towards a great fallen willow whose branches arched over forming a green cave. Inside the still interior they sat reflectively for a while astride the lowest branches while the old man smoked. The brook rippled and gurgled over the stones near by, and the long slender leaves of the willow rustled overhead. Somewhere, higher up the bank, there was the sound of water dripping from a spring in the ferns. May ran her fingers over the velvet moss which grew over the willow trunk, pressing her face close to smell the sweet dankness. In the half light of the tree's umbrella the moss reflected green on her waxy skin. A shadow moved swiftly over them. Looking up they saw a heron plane down in eerie silence and perch on the top-most branch. May stretched out an arm towards Matt, her brown burning eyes themselves like the eyes of a startled bird. He squeezed her hand, pressing a finger to his lips. The old man followed their eyes upwards. Grinning inanely he put two fingers in his mouth and gave a piercing whistle. The great bird rose silently like a piece of ash floating over a bonfire, and reared away as noiselessly as it had arrived while the children roared out of the green cave and stood on the slabs in the middle of the stream calling, waving their arms and flapping till the heron passed out of sight.

A young couple strolling arm in arm nearby stood still in their tracks listening to the commotion. The young man pulled his girl close to him, deeper into the thicket, fondling the downy hair on the nape of her neck, lightly brushing her lips with kisses. The girl hesitated, "Not 'ere Reg, they'll come across us, sure as 'ouses."

He sank to the ground, pulling her towards him. May's eldest brother had grown heavy and straight. No longer a sapling youth, he towered over his brothers, handsome and well girt like a bullock, his mother said, sensing the danger in his heavy frame, thick shoulders and arms and those gentian eyes. But as far as she knew, Reg was still an untried boy, those hands had never yet grasped a trembling girl by the shoulders or cupped a face towards him in the shadow of the aspen leaves.

He teased her taffeta scarf away and lay it on the ground beneath her head, stroking and splaying her loosened hair out into a sweet smelling fan.

The sounds of the children playing in the stream came nearer. Reg quickly rose to his knees, one hand cupped over the girl's mouth, the other carefully drawing down a branch to clear the view of the bank. He saw the flash of a pale cotton dress as May, barelegged, ran up the slope over the knarled tree roots followed by Matt and the other children scrambling behind. The old man picked his way along the stepping stones and went out of sight, calling back to the others to follow.

They crashed through the bracken on the far side of the thicket and rolled round in the foxtail grass underneath the birch trees, damp cobwebs clinging to their faces and burrs in their hair.

The girl quivered beside Reg, as hypnotised by fear as a hen thrush startled in a covert. She held her breath till the sounds trailed away and there was only the smell of trampled earth left in the air. Her fists unclenched and she brushed away the brittle fragments of leaves from her palms.

There was a long walk ahead for the children and Old Man Drew. Part of the way was easy walking along a deep drive through the wood where timber was stacked at intervals beside the cart track. Then they came to a dirt road which led high up over pasture land. Curlews and lapwings flew up from the growing corn in droves and coasted in the high currents of air as the group, huddled together against the north wind, strode towards the hamlet over the next brow.

Reg lay with his arms around the girl for a long time after the playful sounds had receded into the higher reaches of the wood, listening to her breathing, feeling her heart beating against his throat. She had turned away her head and closed her eyes, pretending to be asleep. He went along with her sham and did not disturb her, but she was aware of the urgent rhythmic message from his groin pressed into her thigh. He eased his arms free and propped himself on an elbow watching and waiting. Soon her breathing calmed, she stretched and arched her back, meeting his gaze.

Their hands and lips found each other, pliant and yielding, forcing their way hungrily into the skin, clenching and grasping in sudden release of their daring. The girl swiftly turned over and lay squirming on his chest, pulling his shirt away while a terrifying heat ran through his body. He found the creamy flesh of her breast with his mouth and sucked deep into her, forcing his hard probing fingers down her back and her belly till they met between her thighs, feeling for the first time the secret centre of her ripe young body. She burned to be taken and pushed down towards his hands, a silent scream forming in her throat. A dark swimming rush of blood seared them as they rose facing each other on their knees, ripping at their clothes. They fell in the dried leaves entwining their bodies, searching and devouring while she flailed her arms and ran deep grooves down his naked back.

Fear overcome, they returned like primitive hunters, his weight bearing her down into the ground till she quivered and shook like the aspen. He rose and fell on her, lunging and tearing again wildly, head thrown back, then suddenly crumpled and fell away to the side.

She curled her knees up, flushed and burning, looking across at him spreadeagled on his belly. He was still for a moment, then he turned on his back and cried out loud, laughing up into the trees overhead.

Old Man Drew and the children rested for a while leaning on a gate. As far as the eye could see, the patchwork of fields led on across the plain, blackened here and there by stacks and furnaces whose smoke palls spread into a haze over the landscape. A canal glinted in the distance, and far away a reservoir backed by fir plantations shone like a blot of silver paint.

Soon they were climbing over a stile which led them towards a stone farmhouse in a hollow. The old woman bent at work in the low-walled garden looked up and waved as they approached. Drew's sister was the last remaining member of the family at the old homestead, eking out a living from her few animals and garden produce.

She came, gaunt-faced, to open the gate. Toothless and walnut-skinned, bent in a permanent stoop, she muttered and clacked her tongue, shuffling her boots on the cinder path. The old man shouted his greeting in her ear, winking at the children where they stood apart in a shy little group. She hobbled across, her blackened hand outstretched to pat their heads, then suddenly whirled and shooed them like so many chickens towards the house.

The well water in the jug was the faintest green but tasted refreshingly cool, and the kitchen smelled of mint and cucumber. A vast clock in the corner ticked loudly and a kettle on the grate stood hissing as the children sat quietly at the chenille covered table. She delved in the larder and brought out celery in a cut glass dish, cheese, and a glass of gooseberry wine for Drew.

The children were tired after the long walk and in awe of the old lady, but she prodded them and pushed the food forward encouraging them to eat. They began slowly, nibbling and fidgetting. However, they soon found their appetites and the nodding old lady fetched a basket of wizened apples which she put on the hearth rug for them to munch around the fire.

The children crept out after a while to explore the farm, leaving the old lady dozing in her chair. Nettles, thistles and dock had invaded the neglected yard but over the drystone wall there were a few cultivated patches where she had managed to keep them at bay. Wallflowers drooped from a disused trough and rhubarb stood up scarlet in overturned galvanised buckets. Nearby, a few square yards of fine tilth held fragile young tomatoes and marrows surrounded by a wicket fence draped in hessian.

Old Drew had untied the lurcher from his kennel and was looking for rats. The barn door stood open revealing the long disused machinery which had rusted under the gaping corrugated roof, piles of oil drums and empty feed sacks. Decay ran over the roofs and down the ragstone walls into the rotted timbers and broken floors. The old man tutted as he wandered through the dereliction.

There had been a time when the farm supported a large family, when it had been loved and well husbanded. Now it was too late, too remote from those far off days of his boyhood when a proud rooster crowed in the trim orchard and heifers nuzzled in the warmth of the byre. Even broad backs and strong young arms could not retrieve this wilderness now.

At the end of a muddy track a cob, the last remaining working animal, stood tethered in a paddock.

"Come on you kids," growled Drew, "an' 'elp me get this owd bugger tacked up to t'cart. We'll get yon owd lass and ussens back 'ome in it. Ah don't reckon wi can leave 'er 'ere much longer. Ar missus 'll put 'er up fer a bit. She's too far gone ter stop 'ere."

They led the cob under the lean-to and found the tackle. Drew skilfully harnessed him and backed him into the shafts of the wagon.

"'Ah'll 'ave ter send ar Jack up tomorrow ter kill off owt else. There'll be summat for t'pot anyway. Just stop 'ere a bit an' ah'll go an' get owd lass an' a few o' 'er things."

Evening was falling as they neared the village. A couple were strolling arm in arm through the alders. As the cart crossed the last bridge, May, who was sitting dangling her bare legs over the tailboard, nudged Matt, giggling.

"Look, there's our Reg, 'e's bin out courtin' wi' that Clarice Jackson. Ah waint 'alf pull 'is leg when 'e gets 'ome."

Chapter VI

RASPBERRIES AND KITES

'Matt loves May, Matt loves May
Kiss the girl you love today'.

The two children blushed and ran away often as the others taunted them with their catcall song, unless the girl, who was a year older than Matt felt it in her to swing round and lash out with the end of her skipping rope.

Their lives grew together like fronds of convolvulus as they grew up. May, dark-skinned and bright-eyed, the beautiful urchin who dominated her six brothers, found deep satisfaction in the company of the sturdy fair-haired boy who waited for her every day at the school gate. She had been reared in the Barlow's crowded cottage, surrounded by boisterous lads who threw her about and passed her from knee to knee in a cat's cradle of warmth and affection.

Her mother had found an ally in her only girl, a child that she could draw close and mould to her own likeness. Wearied by the boys, and anxious for the older three who had already followed their father into the colliery workings, Mrs. Barlow comforted herself with May, and treated her like a younger sister from early on. She loved her young men folk deeply, but her survival in the house with its eternal clattering of chairs and cutlery, the endless drawing of water for the tin bath, the singing, bawdy jokes and arguments, depended completely on the bond she made with May. The child sensed her mother's need and responded with easy affection; she grew strong and confident, aware of her responsibilities even at such an early age.

May gave her loyalty also to Matt. He, being an only child sometimes envied the liveliness of other village houses and their almost tangible family ties, but as his friendship deepened with May, their secret understanding drew them together in a web of their own spinning.

On a hot July day the entire school filed out into the garden, the boys to tend their allotments which were planted with neat rows of vegetables and cages of soft fruit, and the girls into the ornamental flower gardens. As the boys tended the plots, hoeing and weeding under the watchful eye of the headmaster, Grannie Horsmann led the girls along the mossy paths and under the pergolas of roses.

Matt watched at a distance. The file of girls, in gingham pinafores sang as they cut lengths of raffia to tie up the clumps of flowers in the herbaceous borders. May, standing between tall, ox-eye daisies, foxgloves and paeonies, her dark hair moving in the warm breeze, waved to him, a cut-out from a book of rhymes. Matt looked away, and quickly knelt down, scratching with his fingers in the dry earth at a tangle of weeds, because it was forbidden to talk to the girls in the garden, and Mr. Miller was patrolling up and down the central path. He coloured at the picture burning in his head of the bare-armed girl swaying in her white apron among the brilliant flowers. Her brown eyes forced his head to turn again, but when he did May was darting silently and low towards him, screened from her classmates by a clump of hydrangeas. Crouching down against the velvet lichen of the path she beckoned Matt.

"Come over 'ere, ah dare thee. Nobody ull see thee. Come on!" she whispered harshly. Like a flash of a bird in a thicket the boy leapt stealthily towards her. She took him by the hand and pulled him into the middle of the thick old beech hedge which bordered the garden.

"What you doin' of? We shan't 'alf get into trouble," Matt whispered anxiously.

"See them raspberries under the netting? Ah want some. Nip in and get me some," she commanded.

"Ah will not, they're all lookin'. Ah don't want ter get caught pinchin'."

She squeezed his arm. "Go on, do as ah tell thee," May pleaded, but there was laughter in her eyes which seized hold of Matt. He parted the leaves, trembling excitedly. The boys were bending down working on their plots and the two teachers were seated on the bench in deep conversation at the other end of the covered walk. Suddenly he ran off towards the fruit cage and scrambled under the net. The ripe raspberries hung in clusters over his head. He stretched up and gently eased away a handful from their stalks. His heart seemed to miss a beat when he noticed with sudden panic the tell tale white cores left behind, which stood out among the carmine fruit as if they had been picked out in luminous paint.

"Somebody will see. They'll notice that," he gasped when he slid back into the hedge.

"Don't mind, they'll never know it were thee. Anyway they could just 'ave fell off, couldn't they?" reasoned May as she lay back in the hollow centre of the leafy hideout, placing the raspberries one by one on her outstretched tongue, savouring the sweet juices. The last one she saved for Matt, but before she popped it in his mouth, she squeezed her eyes tight and ran the berry delicately around her mouth. She leaned forward pouting.

"Ah saw a lady do that at the pictures. And then she kissed the man. But ah shan't do that to you, because we're not old enough. And you're shy. Let's go back."

They wandered through the summer hand in hand when no one was looking, rolling down grassy banks to suck the honey from the clover and dig for pig nuts in a deep confusion of scent and excitement. They played hide and seek among the tall stems of the cow parsley along the hedgerows, scattering the creamy pollen from the lace of the flowers and bruising the hollow stalks into a pungent sweetness.

One day, trailing the kites which village boys had tied off at the very top of the slag-tips and left there to fly through the night, they strolled down the dirt lane, sucking sweets from Mrs. Bedford's jars, towards the old railway bridge and on to the shale-coloured sidings. Up they climbed, the rock slipping under their shoes. May's tangle of curled hair grew damp on her forehead as they climbed higher, skirting the cracks in the tip where sulphurous fumes leaked out and poisoned the air. Once she slipped and started to slide alarmingly down the tip. Matt called out and ran after her, causing a flock of starlings to rise up whirling from the corn field below. They climbed again, resting occasionally on a big rock until they reached the top where the rails pointed out into the sky and the kites flew soaring above them.

As the sun beat down and gusts of wind buffeted around them, they fought to get their breath back in the shelter of some rusted coal tubs abandoned on the slag. The wind dried their upturned faces as they watched the kites clattering their paper tails over the furrows of the decayed landscape and the enormous weaving shadows which they threw from high in the plummeting blue sky down into the valley.

Clinging hold of the top-most cable, Matt pulled himself up to stand astride a girder. He swayed in the rushing air, calling out to the dancing kites.

"This is the top of the world," he shouted, "It makes you want to fly. Climb up, come on, I'll hold on to you."

As May struggled to haul herself up, a great piece of shale slid loose and began to fall. They watched it gather speed, rolling down the tip. It bounced and jerked into the air and whirled on down smashing it's way to the very bottom where with a sickening crash it broke into smithereens on a pile of railway sleepers.

The children both stared down. A trickle of small stones and grit was still sliding below them and threatening to turn into an avalanche.

Matt swung towards May carefully and led her underneath a projecting girder where they sat down and rested. As the air grew still and colder, the sun began to turn red, falling towards the distant Hardwick Hall on the horizon, and the great windows blazed as if the house had burst into flames. They rose and picked their way down carefully by a different route on the other side of the tip and came into a dark gully where a stream rose from a cave in the side of the spoil. The water ran into a pool of silt and lay still as a black mirror. Matt threw in great lumps of wood and watched them float across the oily surface. An enormous toad, which had been crouching on an old rubber tyre on the far bank, plopped into the water croaking hoarsely. May squealed in horror and then ran home.

Chapter VII

DIGGING IN

High summer had gone when the fair arrived and set up on the field at the top of the village. All day the children in school turned their faces to the windows in an agony of anticipation, waiting for four o'clock. On the bell they raced up the field, milling around the vans which the showmen were trying to unload. Swarthy men in greasy overalls good naturedly let the boys help with the gaudily painted swinging boats and dodgem cars. The women, hair coiled high and plaited, sporting gold teeth and heavy earrings flashing against their honey coloured skin, carried out baskets of trinkets and dolls from the caravans to display on the shelves as prizes, while the village children raced around rough and tumbling in the scuffed yellow grass whose scent mingled in an intoxicating way with the smell of oil lamps and the petrol driven generator.

It was still a long time till the lights would go on and the music started, so many children hurried home to grab hunks of bread and cheese and beg a few pennies to spend. As the dusk gathered and mist began to roll across the field, the first flares were lit and coloured lights glowed on overhead wires. The organ crashed out its gaudy rhythm over crackling loudspeakers as the roundabouts turned and the boys jerked the swinging boats high into the air making young girls yell with delight.

Matt and May sat on the steps of a caravan trying to eavesdrop on the fortune teller who was doing a fair trade with the miner's wives. They wondered what best to do with their few coppers, but meanwhile it was good to watch the swirling machinery and the lights brilliantly reflected on the engraved glass and brass curlicues of the vans. Soon the men began to arrive from the public house on the other side of the road, some already swaying heavily with beer bottles in their grasp.

Jess Bedford came by with a group of his mates. He spotted his boy and yanked him on his shoulder. May ran alongside as they made their way to the coconut shies where Matt and his father shared a round or two, winning a goldfish in a bowl. She got treated by a burly farm worker to a ride with him on the dodgem cars from which she screamed and waved frenziedly.

The night wore on, the crowds getting denser and more elated as they jostled about the field, eating hot pies and faggots, washed down with sarsparilla and dandelion and burdock. There was no thought for tomorrow as the village women strolled about arm in arm indulging the children with a a few more coins when they pleaded for another ride.

But a chill wind blew up and gradually the field thinned. Lights came on in the windows of the village houses for the last time that year.

The next morning after the feast most people got off to a late start. Matt was sitting in Mrs. Drew's kitchen waiting for the old man to take him for their usual Sunday walk with the dogs and the ferrets into the gorse. Evelyn had called in for a mug of tea half way round her morning paper delivery, and sat reading with Matt at the table while Mrs. Drew swept the floor in preparation for the day. She clacked her teeth in irritation at the morning's sounds. The wireless hummed and scratched as Jack fiddled with the leads of the wet battery, trying to bring the radio to life, and the old lurchers growled and fought over the enamel feeding bowl.

Old Man Drew came in with the ferrets bulging in his overcoat pockets just in time to hear the announcement. He stood by the varnished sideboard, a curious vacant expression in his watery eyes, his lower unshaven jowl quivering and moist.

After the terrible news had been given out Mrs. Drew sat down in the rocking chair in front of the fire. She had lost three brothers in the First World War and fretted now about her young Jack and the other lads of the village having their turn. It all would seem so far away again, these boys trampling and dying in the mud for the sake of a few old fields. Now, our fields, she mused, as she stared out over the half curtain to the newly ploughed furrows beyond the first copse, that would be different. A flock of rooks swarmed high over the freshly turned earth, and a pair of jet black crows flapped noisily in search of carrion.

Yes, she would send them out there herself if it came to that, and death would be the same, the blood and the shattered bone, staring eyes and torn flesh, but she would at least be able to draw her own young man under a hawthorn bush and bury him in sight of his home.

The long silence that hung round the kitchen was interrupted by a sudden swathe of noise as a train rushed through the cutting, rattling the cracked pane in the window frame.

"They'll all be off soon," said the old man, "Jammed in them carriages wi' their snap tins and their knap-sacks. Theer'll only be us owd uns left. They'll all 'ave ter go, they allus do. Better be off 'ome young Matt, thi mam'll be looking for thee."

Matt tore out of the house, dry in the mouth and trembling as he ran. The church bell up on the hill clanged out and the colliery siren joined in with its high pitched wail, a sound that was especially eerie, being foreign to a Sunday, and too reminiscent of those other times it told of disaster below the ground. The sounds of banging doors and feet running over cobblestones echoed down the rows as neighbours hurried to knock up the late risers who came frightened to their bedroom windows.

The boy paused for a moment to watch the awesome cloud of steam from the siren as it rose and drifted up the valley. As he bolted through the Bedford's back gate and up the steps into the living room, his father was pulling on his rough working clothes and boots.

"You stop 'ere with yer mam an' 'elp 'er get dinner ready, lad," he said. "Ah expect thar's 'eard summat. It'll all be summat or nowt, but we'll 'ave to mek do, shan't we? We're in for a bloody rum time though, ah can tell thee."

He strode out of the house towards the garden shed to collect tools, and went to join the other men of the village who had congregated as if by instinct under the elm on the top field.

The gaudy fairground was littered from the night before, and a few mangy dogs ran round barking at the intruders as they marched out into the middle of the field. The showmen had already started to pack up, and the tawny women were stowing away their tinselled bric-a-brac in packing cases.

The miners hauled the caravans away to the roadside, and soon were at work digging trenches the length of the field. They sang at the tops of their voices, wielding pick and shovel to expert purpose. The sides of the trenches were shored up as quickly and securely as galleries in the pit, then roofed over and camouflaged with turves. The work was helped on by cheering boys who ran off to the public house for beer, and the women came up bantering with jugs of hot tea.

It was almost another gala day.

Chapter VIII
THE FIRST TO GO

At the first ebb of the year, lush meadows were lain and the fruit parted from the leaf in dusky paddocks. Furtive spiders saw their webs hung with the first frosts of autumn, while on the hedgerows blackberries cascaded over the haws. The grass in lanes remained wet and straggled, starred with the last pennymoons, in the penetrating damp which the weak sun failed to clear. Children picked their way through thickets in search of hazel nuts and wild damsons, armed with sticks and dock leaves against the overhanging nettles.

The earth seemed to lay still and exhausted after the harvest which had shaved the fields into geometrical patterns of stubble, and over the gardens hung the incense of burning leaves.

It was a good time for the Yates boys and their dogs. There were partridge and hares in the gorse, fat rabbits in the warren and trout in the ponds over by Sutton Scarsdale.

The village stayed out late in the evenings, enjoying the very last of the weather before the decline into winter, and the children played in the field behind the inn long after twilight while the glare of gas mantles spilled through the chinks in the blackout material spread over steamed-up windows.

At midnight the Yates would still be treading stealthily home, untying the last of their snares and padding barefoot down the cobbled yard.

In October Jess Bedford bought himself a pony and cart in the market place in Chesterfield and began plying his way to surrounding villages and farms with a load of goods from the shop. Sometimes Matt went along with him, perched on an upturned box under the tarpaulin. They feasted on damp sandwiches by the roadside and drank the beer in quiet little pubs far out in the county where Jess had never ventured before.

Mr. Bedford bartered his goods over gateways in neighbouring hamlets, coaxing eggs, honey and home-made cheeses from weather-worn countrywomen; foods which they could continue to supply if the war dragged on and shortages came.

When they unloaded the purchases back at the shop Ma Bedford would hurry out to her son and lead him in to a warm supper by the fire, beaming at his excited stories, pleased with his healthy glow from the fresh air.

The autumn nights became darker, and Jess fixed lanterns to the cart for the journeys home. In the mornings, leaving the house after the first radio news, they would pass men waiting for the early shift, who stood in silent companionable groups at the head of the pit yard, stamping their boots and blowing into their hands. There was, by tradition, little conversation as they waited for the cage to take them hurtling down the shaft. They were resting themselves before the long day in the seam. The war seemed a long way off and they had their own dangers to face.

The first of the boys to join up was Reg, the Barlows' wildest boy. Madge cried hard when they had all gone off to work and May was at school. She and Frank had sat listening to the clock ticking and the cinders falling in the grate for a couple of bitter hours after Reg had put the buff call-up paper behind the caddy on the shelf and gone out whistling. But she waited till the house was empty before she unlatched the door to the staircase to cry into the void.

In a terrifying nightmare she stood alone in a desolate moorland. Icy rivers flowed from her breasts and her mouth over the bannister. Her head was bound by the claws of serpents which drew her upwards to the top of a flat rock from where she could see lines of marble crosses stretching to a fiery horizon. A vast figure entered through the landing window and winged down the stairs towards her, first translucent and weightless, carried by great currents of air and the stench of burning, then becoming barbed and metallic, propelled by explosions of sulphur and lime. The head of the figure shrank into the form of a grey embryo trailing veins which spiralled outwards. It had unborn blind eyes which flickered open and smiled at her. She travelled towards and through them, her body dividing into two equal parts which floated over a field of smouldering wheat. Gripping the window-sill she saw the two halves drawing towards each other like giant silken bats across a limitless sky of the purest rose. They joined together again, dissolving into a faded photograph with torn edges which crumbled into fine ash and sparks dancing on flames in a chimney.

Her hands tore at the drawers in the chest upstairs till she found a tin box stuffed with old letters, postcards and snapshots of rare holidays. Frank with May on his shoulders at the Sunday School outing in Skegness, and Reg sitting on a motor bike in the booth by the beach at Mablethorpe, his fringe cut straight across the forehead, a cap stuck on top, and the old brown jersey with the fair isle pattern she had knitted while waiting for one of them.

Miles of thick wool travelled through her fingers past her worn wedding ring as she fell crumpled on the mattress and unravelled out into the street festooning the electric cables, while the slates of the houses opposite burst in deafening screams and lay in piles around her white-washed doorstep.

The neighbours on both sides pressed their ears to the thin walls and cried silently with Madge and stroked her greying hair with their knotted hands in a pain which bore through the plaster. Outside, dogs ran barking through the yards, skirmishing the clouds of soap and disinfectant that rose from the open drains, while turbaned heads rolled and sighed over the green gates.

May banged down her desk lid and sat bolt upright in her chair in the vaulted schoolroom as the tide of anguish ran from her mother. The class turned towards her and trembled at the deathly pallor which drained her face.

Beyond the open window men were tramping down the gantry, hurrying for home. It would soon be time for school to close, she thought numbly and uncomprehending through the last remorseless minutes of the wall-clock.

Mrs. Barlow shuffled across the kitchen in her felt slippers and poked the fire. They would all be in soon, in a while they would all be in. Familiar singing got nearer down the alley.

Reg home from town on the four o'clock bus with his new suitcase and some brown paper parcels. The others coming in one by one, dropping their water bottles and belts behind the door. Water splashed in the enamel bowl and boots thrown in the cupboard. Hollow sounds from the well of the pantry; bread bin and carving knife, tap running, the kettle boiling over the hob. Newspaper spread out on the table. Move those feet, the coal bucket's empty. May, be a love and get the washing in. Can you see your dad on the lane? Will you be wanting some tea Reg before you're off? Tea in the pot and the buff paper on the mantlepiece. A pile of mending on the settle under the window. Smooth the apron, cut the bread. Reg coming downstairs with his new case packed. They'll all be up the field soon to see him off. The walk down the hill in town to the station. The station sliding away back down the line, the train vanishing into a tunnel. Sit down all of you. Pass these plates round. Well Reg, we'd better start or you'll miss your bus. Oh, here comes your Dad. I thought it would be nice if we all had tea together.

He'll come back soon. They give them leave to come home and see their mothers, perhaps he'll only be gone a few days. Let's start then. Reg hand me your cup, luv. Later I'll do the sheets off his bed and put them away wrapped in clean tissue paper with some sweet smelling stuff. Then I'll do his shirts and collars and put them away in my cupboard so the others don't get at them. When the water's hot I'll drop in a blue bag and squeeze it and swill it round till the water's blue, and dip his things in to make them fresh and clean for him. They'll never know how I went up the stairs and cried like a baby this afternoon. They'll never know it tore my heart out when he told me he was going, and I wished it were any of them, anybody else but my Reg, the one who shines out for me, with his lovely eyes and those great arms he puts round me when the others aren't looking. Thank God I've still got my May and she'll never leave me. She won't be called away like Reg. God, I wish it were one of the others. A few more minutes. I'll leave the washing up and tell him it's time for his bus. I'll see him off up the street. He'll wave at the corner and that's the last I'll ever see of him. He'll never come back.

A good half of the village turned out to see Reg off. The bench under the elm tree opposite the bus stop was taken up quite early by half a dozen old men who no longer worked and had plenty of time on their hands. The other men, miners, farm labourers and Reg's young mates who worked with him on the pit top all had to wash and have their tea, so they strolled up a little later, chaffing the women. Several bent grey-haired ladies who normally got no further than Ma Bedford's shop half way up the hill decided it was a nice day, and the first one to go deserved a good send-off.

Mrs. Bedford did not care to close the shop before the late afternoon shift was over for that would have spoiled things for the last few coming up in the cage wanting cigarettes. But she sent Matt up the road with a carrier bag filled at random with things from her packed shelves; sweets, a swiss roll, some socks and handkerchiefs.

Daredevil girls leaned cheekily on their bicycles promising themselves that they would write Reg silly letters to cheer him.

"Do we get a kiss Reg? You can't go off and leave us like that, love."

"Oh, 'e's blushing. Come 'ere, duck, yer know I'm your favourite."

"You'll look smashin' in yer uniform, kid, bet the girls ull all be after yer."

"Tar rah, duck, bye Reg, don't forget to write."

The bus lurched off followed by a crowd of running boys. Reg waved from the back seat and was soon lost to sight at the turn in the road.

May stayed out with Matt long after the crowd split up. They sat on the bench looking towards the west and a glimmering salmon sky.

She shivered a little and pulled her cardigan tight round herself.

"I can't believe it, our Reg going like that. Just gone. I wonder when we'll see him again," she said quietly.

Matt said nothing in reply. She seemed to want no answer.

Far away, ahead of them, the sky took on different colours of orange and gold as the evening drew in and the light of distant furnaces tinged the lowest clouds.

The bus would by now be near town and Reg would be reaching for his case from the rack. The train would draw in and take him further west into the city and beyond.

A breeze blew across the road making the children want to draw nearer to each other. But they stayed apart, leaning their elbows on the rail of the bench, lost in each other's thoughts.

Matt turned his head towards May and saw tears falling freely down her cheeks. He had to turn away again because a tight feeling that came in his throat threatened to well up in his own eyes. He scuffed in the ground, bit his thumb and concentrated very hard on some small crack in the wood of the bench, picking at it now and then with a finger nail, in order to summon up the courage to speak with a steady voice.

"Shall we go for a walk tomorrow, May? I know where there's some sweet chestnuts in the wood."

Then, with a rush, "Don't cry, May, I can't see you cry like that. Stop now!"

May drew her knees up, burying her chin in the folds of her skirt, wide-eyed at the deepening sunset; and Matt, his hands thrust in his pockets, leaned forward, drawing patterns in the dust with his heels.

The headlights of an occasional car or lorry coming up the hill stabbed into the air like probing fingers and caught her in silhouette, crouched forward in a rocking motion which gradually seemed to calm her, but Matt's own feelings ran around uncontrolled and wayward as the scuffles he was making in the dirt.

The silence between them lengthened and ran out across the fields towards the glow from the furnaces, and the first stars pointed quiveringly in the sky. There was a feeling of great distances and bitterness in the waning spaces beyond the plumes of the blue trees.

He turned to her and felt the need to comfort her. His arm crept towards her and passed round her shoulder. She turned and smiled, ruffling the wisps of hair from her forehead.

"Aven't we sat 'ere a long time, ah've got real chilled, ah think we'd best be goin' in."

They rose from the bench and walked back down the track towards the village. Halfway down Matt faced her.

"Look, May, I don't understand about war and things and you don't either. I wish they'd tell us what it's all about."

And, after a pause, "Dad says a lot more will 'ave to go, but they won't mind. Look 'ow your Reg went off laughing. Come on, let's go 'ome, it's cold."

As they parted to go their different ways they called out to each other, their voices echoing rent the gennils.

Chapter IX

NEWSPAPER CUTTINGS

When discreet enquiries had been made by the village constable, and the district nurse had sent in her report, Clarice Jackson's mother packed a suitcase and took her daughter to stop with Aunt Sarah at Newark. She stayed long enough to see her settled in her new job in a munitions factory before she came home leaden-hearted.

Behind the caddy on the shelf was the cutting Ted had taken from the county newspaper. A short factual account; grievous, she thought, all their lives sewn up and bound into a couple of grey paragraphs next to the Whist Drives and the Chrysanthemum Show.

Neighbours were kind and stayed away. No-one talked about the affair after Ma Bedford had put an embargo on the gossip in the shop. It was private, she said, a closed book and Millie Jackson would eat her heart out for ever. They'd all better look to their laurels, hadn't they? She wondered what else had gone on and nobody knew about. That poor kid, she'd only done what came to her head when she was reckless and desperate. If only she'd told her, or told her own mam, it needn't have come to this. Dead flowers rotting in the cemetery up the hill, the awful clang of the first bell on Sundays to remind you of the old rector leading the procession towards the oozing clay. Life would go on, but the hideous memories, the images burnt into the mind, and the savage waste and misery of it all. The poor child on her own in the privvy across the back yard, pain, still birth, guilt and shaking terror of discovery. How to clean up all traces of the blood and mess, scrabbling with rags and floor-cloths? Wrap the gaunt little thing up in newspaper and carry it parcelled inside her overcoat along the top road away from the village, past the last houses and lights, the barbed wire, the cleated hedge and the ditch.

They brought the newspaper months later to Jess Bedford after a farm labourer sheltering from the sleet stumbled reeling numb with sickness away from the ditch. In the top corner of the front page there was the number of the Jackson's house in Bedford's own writing. He shook his head, lying, gently bullied by the constable, but the truth will out, blurting into walls, skirtings and dados, light spinning from mirrors and the brass fender.

Afterwards, he took the poker to the grate, staring through the flames to the fireback.

Reg, poor Reg, he thought, pride and cracker of the row, perhaps he'll die in a blast of iron, spilled like so much clinker. The rain and leaves will cover him in a culvert and he'll never know how the courting in the woods ended.

Chapter X
DAYS OF REST

Sundays for the Bedfords brought few surprises. If the Lord's Day were meant to be a rest, that must be for other folk, the lady of the house had decided, a sop for the work-shy and the feckless. She brooked no such consideration and attacked the day as if it could be her last on earth, knowing there would be no peace in heaven for her if, by the end of it, there was one iota of muck, one skerrick of dirt, an unwanted crease, scratch on the furniture, unpressed collar or holed sock.

By six o'clock she had the boiler humming and her wash soaking in the tub. Her singing woke Jess and Matt who both stumbled down for tea.

"Get your own," she would shout over the suds, "Ah can't stop just now, ah'll just pan out if ah keep goin'."

They sighed because she meant all day. On a cold morning Evelyn also would get a cup, or in summer a quick glass of homemade lemonade from the pantry.

"Come on, you shirkers, these papers is all in my way," she would cry, gathering the half finished cups, "Mek yerselves scarce an' give me some elbow room."

While the three delivered the Sunday newspapers, the washing would be strung up on the line, the fire raked and lighted, and the lav down the yard fettled out.

"Can't 'ave no breakfast, not before communion, thar'll 'ave ter sing on an empty stomach and thank God thar's got a good 'ome ter come back to, duck, what can give thee a plate o' good grub," she reasoned with Matt who came back famished from his round.

"Now, Evelyn, come upstairs with me and we'll go through t'drawers and pull out anythin' what wants freshening up." She proceeded to rewash, starch and iron curtains, pillowcases and bedspreads which were pristine clean but had lain idle a bit too long for her liking.

"Ah shall feel better when they've had a good blow, never liked mucky drawers."

She ran a fresh bowl of soapy water for Matt to wash his breakfast things after church.

"While you're at it, luv, just reach up and get mi best pots down an' gi'e 'em a swill," indicating row after row of china, cut glass, sherry glasses, vases and her favourite tea-pot shaped like a racing car with a goggled driver's head for a knob.

"What about a bit o' bakin' nah," she grinned at Ev, donning a clean apron and scrubbing her hands in gleeful anticipation.

"'Ave ter get it in afore t'dinner can get started, can't be goin' two things at once, can we?"

Flour sifted, sleeves rolled up, tins greased, mixtures whisked, kneaded, pummelled, plaited, pricked and cajoled into shape. Jam and mincemeat spooned, dessicated coconut and nutmeg shaken, apples cored, chocolate grated, rapture in her eyes and her face crimson from the heat of the range.

"That should just about see us through t'week," when there was a shelf groaning with enough cakes and pies to feed an army.

"Ev, you run this rag wi' t'linseed over t'polished furniture, while ah make a start on mi greens, an' Matt be a good lad an tek a duster to t'stairs, don't miss no corners."

"Nice bit o' shinbeef, this, it'll go down well wi' a few carrots and cauli, some broad beans, taters, peas and onion sauce."

"Better fetch yer dad now, 'e'll be 'avin' a jar. Or thar'll be late for Sunday School."

"Come on, Ev, while we waitin' we can gi'e t'shop floor a swill an' do some stockin' up. Bit of a dust round, we'll 'ave it shunklin' like a little palace."

"Oh yer 'ere. Thought you'd gone for t'duration. Get stuck in while it's 'ot."

"Best you clear up, Ev, while ah start on t'ironing, then ah want them net curtains down."

"Nearly four o'clock and that lad not back, an' why aren't thar shaved? Thar knows 'arriet's expectin' us."

"Come on lad, nip on an' tell t'bus ter wait fer yer owd mam."

"Well, ah never, look 'oos 'ere, well, ah never."

Auntie Harriet, garrulous and over excited, Cousin Mavis and Uncle Fred. Tea and fairy cakes, then Mavis singing Chirri Chirri Bin, Roses of Picardy, The Pipes of Pan followed by Matt rendering Oh for the Wings of a Dove, Where ere you Walk, Jess and Uncle Fred doing Mi Father Painted the Parlour, Ole Man River, Trees, and Mam and Aunt Harriet finishing off with When you Come to the End of a Perfect Day.

Home to Albert Sandler at the Grand Hotel and Lillian Duff in Continental Cabaret.

"There must be some 'omework you've not finished. Then yer can 'elp me wi' these bills. No peace fer t'wicked."

"Up them apples an' pears, goodnight, 'ope the bugs don't bite."

Chapter XI

PRIVATIONS

No-one was more pleased than Grannie Horsmann when the workmen arrived to start on the fancy new water closets. She had made a log over the years of the epidemics of scarlet fever, mumps, chicken pox, measels, worms, whooping cough and dyptheria that had laid her classes low, and she blamed the old earth closets. There were times when the entire school was shaved, painted in gentian violet, covered in alarming spots, or wracked by hideous coughs. The dame wrinkled her nose when she had occasion to pass by the rows of privvies and beat a way through clouds of bluebottles with her umbrella. What was the use, she thought, trying to instill the basic precepts of hygiene to these children in her cloakrooms when the facilities at home were so primitive.

There were just a few very old ladies saddened at losing the old thrones, especially the two-holers. What could be more civilised than a pleasant stroll down the yard with a good neighbour and the cheering prospect of a ruminative half-hour in the warm privacy of the closet? Cut off from the cares of the kitchen, prying ears and eyes, tally men, sugar borrowers and other irritating interferences, the privvy was the ideal spot for chewing the fat.

There was probably more reading done in the cloistered quiet of these premises than in any other part of the local households. If nothing of great depth, there would be plenty of good browsing material; Red Letter, John Bull, Old Moores Almanack and Harry Wheatcroft's catalogue of roses. Failing all else, one could leaf through random selections of torn-up newspaper squares hanging from a nail on the back of the door.

"Please Mrs. Bedford, mi mam wants a roll of lav paper."

"'Ere you are, duck, mind yer change, nah, there's a good lass."

Later that day.

"Ah'm sorry Mrs. Bedford, mi mam says can yer tek this back, an' can she 'ave the money, mi auntie's not coming to see us after all."

It became obvious that the scale of the work involved was going to throw the village into a turmoil.

"It'll be no picnic," Mrs. Lakinshawe said sadly, thinking of the upheaval to come when she spied the surveyors measuring up.

"Still, we 'ave ter move wi' t'times, don't we?"

"It'll be like livin' in a stately 'ome," declared Mrs. Lawton, "Folk ull be payin' soon to come an' view. Roll up, roll up, ah shall be sayin', this way ter t'waterworks, mind yer put yer macs on."

The old closets had been an eyesore, in spite of the liberal use of lime and whitewash, and an affront to the nostrils as long as anyone could remember. In cold spells when there was plenty of fire-ash to throw over the waste, things were mildly in control, but on a hot midsummer day a trip down the yard had to be fleeting and woebetide the constipated.

On Friday nights Bert Raybould stomped down the alleys on his wooden leg, leading the shire which pulled the scabrous shit-cart. The creak of the ancient vehicle, accompanied by the clip-clop of hooves and the rhythmic tapping of Bert's crutch and stump on the cobbles drove the children indoors. They listened fearfully to the bolts being drawn, the back doors of the hovels being thrown open and the clang of the shovel as Bert performed his hideous duties.

He had lost a leg many years before in a flying drum of vicious cable down below and now he was the untouchable who came at night when the curtains were drawn; he was the bogey man who would throw a bad child into the sludge and cart him away to a stinking dump in the nettles.

The next morning women would peer through their curtains to see if it was all clear for them to run across with buckets of water and a broom to do the remaining ablutions in the backs. Somehow that was a job to be done in private.

The work began with a fine swing. Navvies dug deep ditches which intersected the village like a grid. Then they went away and the ditches lay empty and untended for months. Folk had to skirt round them, making detours through alleys and gennils, or attempt perilous crossings on makeshift bridges of swaying planks. Rain and frost eroded the banks, and old ladies slipped in the ooze dreading the onset of another nasty bout of lumbago. The odd infant finished up squawling face down in the clay after being catapulted out of its pram and the child in charge got well clouted by its hysterical mother.

If the ditches filled with water kids sailed paper boats in them, and when they froze over they jumped in and made slides. From a distance it was as if they had disappeared except for their balaclava'd heads which whizzed along like so many travelling teapot knobs.

A fat lad thought one day he was Donald Campbell breaking a world record as he pedalled his rusty bike downhill, working up enough steam to launch himself up and over the divide, but although he puffed and yelled himself into a delirium the pull of gravity proved too much and he fell with a sickening thud, still astride the saddle, and blacked out at the monstrous screaming pain in his nethers.

The new conveniences were a long time coming, but it was worth the waiting when a lorry arrived with a load of shining white porcelain basins packed in straw, and a van stacked with polished lav seats, cisterns, piping and chain pulls.

Mrs. Lawton strolled up to the field when all the goods had been unpacked and laid out in neat rows.

"'Ang on a minute lads, just you wait till ah've tried em all aht. Ah want my name on a good un, ah'm not 'avin' nowt what's not a good fit."

Laughing gleefully, she squatted on a few pans.

"Bloody 'ell, they're all t'same."

The men lolled in the straw eating their snap, guffawing at her antics.

"Standard size, missus," one called.

"Well, yer can tek 'em back then, there's no two arses t'same, is theer now. Look at mine, lad, all puckered and withered, an' there's some buggers wot's got backsides like sows. My owd man's the size of an 'ippopotamus, 'e wouldn't get near owt like this bloody little piss-pot, an' ah'm that scrawny ah'll 'ave ter watch out ah don't flush mesself down t'ole."

The great day came. Everything was fitted, connected, the water main turned on, and the new sewerage farm behind the pit tips waited the first discharge.

Mrs. Lawton called to her neighbours.

"Are yer all present an' correct so ah can get on wi' this do?"

She walked across the yard towards her sparkling new lav and faced her mates. She held a rolling pin upright and wore a saucepan lid tied with a piece of string over her bosom.

"As Lady Mayoress of this parish I am about ter christen this new bog."

Giving a spirited account of 'Onward Christian Soldiers' she marched into the privvy and proceeded to do her duty. There were cheers and a round of applause when she opened the door and in full view pulled the chain.

The ladies doubled up and screeched, tears rolling down their cheeks as Mrs. Lawton roared to be heard over the triumphant cascade from the cistern.

"I name thee the Queen Mary. God bless this bog an' all that shit in 'er."

Chapter XII

MISSING THE PICTURES

Ma Bedford eased back the coverlet. She had been only half-asleep for hours, worrying about getting up in time to catch the first workmen's bus into town, and it nagged her that the shop would be closed all day while she was over at Killamarsh for Bella's wedding.

"Nice girl, Bella," she said more or less to herself as she fixed her stays.

"T'least ah can do is ter go ovver and put mi face in when she's one o' mi own flesh an' blood, though ah don't see that side much these days, them livin' that far an all, isn't it, duck? Nah shake thissen, Jess, what's thar think? Ah mean it seems a reight ter-do goin' off an' leavin' ev'rybody wi'out so much as a loaf, it bein' Saturday. They'll all be round Sunday mornin', ah'm tellin' thee. 'Ead's like colanders some on 'em. Gravy salt, custard powder, sponge cakes for trifles, thar'll see."

Jess pulled himself deeper under the covers while she went downstairs and out to the privvy. He had another half-hour before he had to meet the other gangers down on the embankment. They were going far up the line towards Derby to clear a fall of rock in a cutting. With any luck they would be back in time for the kick-off at half past two, or at least the second half.

He could hear Evelyn crooning to herself as she hurried along the gennil and unlatched the sneck of the side gate, and he followed the thuds of the bundles of newspapers as she lifted them on to the kitchen table, then the rattling in the drawer for a knife and the sharp snap of string as she made the cuts.

Soon Ma Bedford was dressed and ready to go, a little breathless for giving Evelyn her marching orders for the day at the same time as straightening her stockings and pinning her hat, the navy-blue felt with red cherries.

"Sithee 'ere luv," she said.

She had managed to find a few tiny smears and splashes around the range and a single finger mark on a window pane, a couple of crumbs under the table, and a jam jar in the pantry that was slightly sticky to the touch.

"They're not much in themselves, luv, but they all add up, don't they," she said encouragingly, dabbing her nose with her rarely used Madame Dubarry puff.

"Don't you dare ter get up to no trouble," she shouted up to Matt, "And no goin' off anywhere till Ev's finished t'papers and made yer breakfast. And mind t'house isn't a pig 'ole when ah get back, or else there'll be ructions. Ah've left thee sixpence on t'sideboard and, does thar 'ear, ah want thee down ter Mr. Kershaw's for an 'aircut. Tell 'im ter tek plenty off while e's at it. Ah'm off luv, tarrah, tarrah Jess."

She stopped for a last look in the low mirror and turned to Evelyn for approval.

"Will ah do?"

"It's a lovely turn out, Mrs. Bedford," the girl said admiringly. "Them duster coats is all t'go nowadays. You're reight in t'fashion. T'three quarter sleeves just shows yer bangle off nice, and navy's very smart".

"Ah got it at Florrie Ford's on Knifesmithgate," Ma Bedford replied, "she only sells models."

Matt sat up in bed after she had gone, working out the best way to spend the sixpence. Twopence for the haircut left twopence for the pictures and twopence for the bus fares. Or whether to walk or bike to Hasland and back and save twopence for chips or buy a penny cream bun and a sherbet. He'd wait until he saw Norman and they could spend the morning deciding.

After his father had gone to work and Evelyn had finished clearing up, Norman came to the gate, whistling with two fingers at his mouth. The boys retreated to the shed in the yard, and over a prolonged swop session trading army buttons and cigarette cards, pondered the question. They finally decided to save some money by walking, since anyway Norman's bike was out of action; one to lash out on a bun and sherbet, the other to buy chips, then share and share alike and get a taste of everything.

The business settled, they began kicking a ball around the yard, using the dog kennel for goal. Evelyn had swilled the flags to shining perfection. She cast a beady eye as she set to on the kitchen window.

"Yer want ter look out," she admonished, "Yer dad ull be furious if 'e knows yer've bin footballin' 'ere when there's t'field ter play in. Tek yerselves off afore there's some damage done."

"'Ere, catch," shouted Matt, throwing the ball.

In a reflex action Evelyn dropped the chamois leather and reached out. The pop crate she was standing on wobbled and she fell shrieking, and the boys stood aghast as the ball sailed past her, smashing the top pane of the window.

Glass flew everywhere, splintering down on Evelyn and into the sink inside the kitchen. The dog roared from his kennel and Mr. Peacock ran out from next door to find out what the commotion was about. He leaned over the privet grinning.

"That's put an end to yer footballin', 'asn't it, yer silly buggers. Just wait till thi dad get's 'ome and finds a gapin 'ole in t'yon window, 'e'll tan thi backside wi' t'buckle end."

The next few moments went by very slowly for the stricken boys. Mrs. Peacock joined her husband at the hedge, rubbing flour from her hands and shaking her head in reproach.

"Look, Jack, they've gone all white in t'gills," she said, "no wonder, wi' what's comin' to 'em later."

Evelyn pulled the bits of glass from her scrimpy curls and sat down on the pop crate to recover herself and evaluate the damage. Norman fetched a broom and began feebly sweeping until Evelyn, more composed now and incensed by the lad's indolence, clouted him across the ear and seized the brush from him.

By now saliva was trickling from her mouth and her eyes were damp with rage. The sweeping up done, the three stood gazing at the window. Peacock went back into his house for his pipe. He returned and leaned crossed-armed over the hedge, puffing.

"Thar's got about four 'ours ter get that shit'ouse put right," he said to Matt, beaming. "That is, unless thi feyther knocks off early. And if 'e does ah wouldn't like ter be in thy shoes."

"What can ah do?" the boy implored, "Ah can't mend it, ah wouldn't know how to start."

"Thar can start by gettin' in my sticks and coal while ah get a chisel, and while thar at it, and that other bloody rogue, ah'll 'ave our midden cleaned up and t'rabbits ferked out. Jump to lads, there's a lot ter get on wi'."

When the idea that Peacock was going to save the day penetrated, the boys were galvanised into action. They tore round the gennil to get into his yard and begin the allotted tasks.

Peacock wandered down the path towards his shed, humming to himself. It was aggravating watching his slow progress.

"Why can't 'e 'urry up," hissed Norman, "Ah think ah'll piss missen if 'e don't soddin' start."

Peacock caught sight of them.

"What yer waitin' on then? Look sharp and don't be so lacksadaisical, ah want nowt slipshod."

The boys quickly hatcheted a pile of sticks and cracked a couple of buckets of coal in record time, then tackled the midden with whitewash and lime. They ran back and stood watching the old man, jiggling on their heels and whistling impatiently under their breaths. He was carefully teasing out the last fragments of glass and chipping away the old putty, pausing now and then to blow a speck away, or prise out a rusty pin. Without turning he said calmly, "Ah want all them sticks put neat in boxes in t'shed, and there's another scuttle you'll find under t'sink in t'kitchen what wants fillin', an' don't ferget them rabbits. Yer can nip up t'field an' get em a bag o' dandelions, an' ar missus 'as got some carrot tops in t'bowl."

They ran off to do as bid, watched by the doleful Mrs. Peacock over her half-curtain and Evelyn sitting in a trance on the upturned crate.

"Ow much 'ave yer got between yer then?" Peacock asked later, inspecting the prepared frame with satisfaction.

"We've both got sixpence from our Mams," Matt replied, "for t'pictures and 'aircuts this afternoon."

"There wain't be any pictures for you buggers nah, will there?" he said impassively, digging Matt in the ribs with his chisel.

"Get yerselves off and see if yer can get a pane and fetch it back wi'out breakin' it. 'Ere's t'measures. A bob wain't do, though. It'll be more'n that."

Evelyn sprang back to life, rushed into the house and came back with eyes blazing. She slapped a shilling into Matt's hand.

"Good job ah got yer mother's wages this mornin' in't it, so ah can rob meself and pay for yer silly muckin' about, yer gormless 'aporth," she screamed. "Nah get off and thank Mister Peacock for all 'is trouble 'e's taken and don't get into any more 'ow d'yer do's, otherwise ah shall be after thee, and that other snotty little arse'ole."

She yanked the hair of the pair of them and flounced out of the gate.

"It's very good of you, Mister Peacock," Matt mumbled, lowering his head, "Ah'll do some more jobs for you when you want."

"Oh ay," Peacock stared back, unimpressed, as the boys sneaked off. After rounding the corner they ran wildfire for a mile before collapsing on a bank by the roadside.

"Thar lucky," said Norman, chewing a blade of grass, "Thar couldn't a' done that thissen. 'E's not so bad, old Peacock pisser. 'E could 'ave just left us to it an' then there'd a' bin murder."

He took out his penknife and idly jabbed it into the ground, tearing at the grass roots. Gradually he worked a hole in the soft loam underneath and poked a finger inside.

"Feel down 'ere," he said.

The earth was warm and soft to the touch inside and there was the scent of crushed plantain.

"As thar ever seen owt like this?" he asked.

Pulling his trousers down to his knees he rolled over on to his belly and guided his prick into the hole.

"This is what men do, only its up women's 'oles, and they bounce up and down ter make babbies. They piss up inside 'em, just like this."

He lay quite still on the bank, arms outstretched, and emptied his bladder into the ground.

"'Ave a go thissen," he urged.

"Nay, not in thy 'ole," Matt retorted, "Ah'll dig out mi own."

The anxieties of the past hour or so receded as the boys gambolled on the bank and exchanged other vital bits of information they had recently gleaned. It was only when the ten o'clock chugged by on the down line sending out clouds of steam as it tackled the sharp gradient that Matt panicked, remembering the errand they were supposed to be running, and dragged Norman to his feet.

They trotted on towards Hasland where the queue for the morning picture show was already forming. They stared jealously at the untidy straggle of children outside the Electric waiting for the doors to open, and at the posters which to their chagrin promised the Dead End Kid, Will Hay and a Tarzan episode.

Reluctantly they crossed over to Willett's Hardware and waited to be served. Through the crowded window display, compounding their agony, they could observe the cinema's doorman unbolt the entrance and usher the queue inside to the kiosk.

The pane, wrapped in newspaper and bound with sticky brown paper tape, cost eighteen pence. They took the sixpence change and sat on the wall outside the shop debating whether they dared, in the circumstances, spend anything on snap. Deciding that they were due for some compensation for missing the flicks, they settled for a bag of chips and a bottle of sarsparilla to be shared. Norman was duly despatched.

Matt stayed on the wall guarding the glass which was propped up nearby. He swung his legs and whistled in pleasureable anticipation of the variety of tastes; hot, salty, vinegar, cold and fruity, until a sudden shock wave of horror struck him just as Norman was coming into view round the corner. He leapt from the wall, missing the pane of glass by inches.

"Let's take 'em back," he yelled, "Maybe she'll give us the money back." But it was too late. Norman already had his face in the bag and the screwtop was off the bottle.

"What are we goin' to do now?"

There was twopence left, and still two haircuts to pay for. One of them was going to get it in the neck.

They gobbled the chips without tasting them and burped on the pop as they hurried toward's Mr. Kershaw's, hoping there would not be too much of a queue waiting.

"'Angin' around t'barbers in't goin' ter get this glass 'ome, yer know what that old fart's like, snippin' and chippin'," Norman complained.

But they were in luck. There was just one old boy having a shave and one nipper waiting. They settled themselves on the horsehair bench and tried to stem their impatience, flicking through a tattered copy of Picture Post, a Lilliput and a John Bull.

Mr. Kershaw followed the old boy to the door and engaged himself in a pleasant conversation, enjoying a breath of fresh air, while the nipper climbed into the chair and knelt waiting for the ordeal to come. The mahogany clock ticked away for what seemed like half a century. He dawdled back, viewing the nipper with some distaste and began tucking the sheet in the lad's jersey. Matt could no longer contain himself. He blurted out his story as Kershaw started the painful attack with the shears. The barber sniffed and tutted disapprovingly, both at the tale and the whimpering nipper, but indicated the broom in the corner and the shorn locks on the floor. He was a man of few words where boys were concerned so he pressed on in silence with the fearful clippers while Matt and Norman swept the floor, then cleaned the engraved mirrors till they sparkled, washed out the basins and polished the shaving mugs. He gave them both a severe short back and sides and a couple of painful nicks which he dabbed with a styptic pencil, drawing tears from their eyes.

They thanked him profusely and set about the walk home. The glass dug into their fingers, even though it was wrapped and they took turns carrying it. Peacock was waiting for them.

"You've tekken long enough, yoh lads, 'ave yer bin mekkin' it?" he growled, ambling into the Bedford's yard.

While he began fixing the pane in place Matt ran into the house to look at the clock. Half-past one. His dad could be back any minute. Peacock expertly ran the putty around the frame. He had just started to stir his paint when the boys heard laughter and shouting coming from the lower end of the street.

The gangers were coming up the hill away from the embankment, jostling, racing for the ball. They came running up the alley, dribbling and heading, over the moon that they were in time for the match.

Jess Bedford was in the middle of the scrum. He trapped the ball and sized up his chance while the others backed away and lunged about waiting for a pass.

Matt and Norman froze, looking imploringly at Peacock poised with his paintbrush.

Jess feinted, dodged, was just about to kick when he noticed Peacock on the step-ladder at the window, two white faced boys, and Mrs. Peacock peering over the hedge.

It was instantaneous, like a snapshot, only a split second, but it threw him, he said afterwards. Jess, the proud footballer, winced when he thought about it; the terrible aim when he was caught off balance and kicked a ball right through his own window.

Chapter XIII
HORSEPLAY

November closed in on the valley with ice cold fog locked between the hills throughout the shortened days, the ground underfoot hard and silver. Washing hung freezing on the lines to the despair of women bent over the fires, and got streaked with soot from the tall stacks in the pit yard. The village seemed cut off from the outside world, and those who ventured into town on market day were marooned shivering on the roadside waiting for late buses.

The nights grew wild in the blackout. After stoking up on baked potatoes, hot-pot and mugs of sweet tea, the children would roar out of the houses through the pitch black alleys in gangs, yodelling and attacking in marauding dangerous games of kick-can and flying horses. They cut their knees and swore themselves hoarse falling over the sharpened flints and drew sparks from the stones with their boots. Their cigarettes glowed at house-ends as they trampelled and shunted about in mysterious rituals, singing lewd songs, wrestling with loud-mouthed girls in porches and electing their gang leaders. They bragged and strutted and marked out their territories. Rival gangs would burst out from the end of a street and hurl stones, then run off down the embankment and hide while the other youths hollered around the alleys in search of a victim by return.

But the men slept unwashed in their fireside chairs, undisturbed by the din and too exhausted after their long shifts to rouse themselves up to the pub.

The women would open their curtains a fraction about seven and peer out, waiting for Mona to clack up the row on her way into town. She wore red wedged-heels and daring blouses even on these chilly nights, holding a filter cigarette to her crimson painted lips as she walked purposefully up to the main road to hitch a lift into town. She would stand there impassively, watched at a distance by the lads, her plucked eyebrows and apricot-powdered face turned towards the traffic, with one foot bound by a narrow ankle strap held forward in invitation. While Mona was busy under the arcade on the top side of the market place, and afterwards in the rear room of the Wine Vaults, her son and daughter held open house. Matt was invited soon by young Brenda into the warm kitchen for the nightly session that was held when the outside games were over.

"Where've you bin?" asked Ma Bedford often when Matt came in late, flushed, making straight for the tap and the flannel to hide his confusion.

"Out playing," he would reply awkwardly.

"What, till this 'our, and in this perishin' cold. Don't let me 'ear of you gettin' into trouble wi' none o' them girls. Ther's some bad lasses round 'ere. Why don't you stop with May? Now she's a good un. Ah wish ah'd a girl like that. Ay, she's a grand un, she'd never get up to no tricks. You watch out, there's a good lad, come 'ere and give your Mam a kiss an' off to bed."

At night, while his mother nodded over her accounts downstairs, Matt curled up in his warm eiderdown, and thought guiltily about May who would surely be ashamed of him and the games in that house with Brenda, her brother Norman and the others. First they made bonfire toffee over the gas ring in old tin trays, and cracked it with a hammer on the brick floor. They sat chewing, reading comics and Old Moores Almanack, played draughts and darts on the back of the pantry door, and the boys pee'd into the stone sink in the corner. But afterwards they fell in a heap on the sofa in the parlour and played the games which Norman, who was the oldest of the boys, had learned down the road earlier that summer. In a marigold infested garden, under the lilac, and screened by tall hedges, children sucked at crusts of bread in the shade. The girls bound their heads with chains of flowers, poppies and creamy privet, and the boys lay watching, plucking at the grass to chew the sweet ends.

They had opened the porch door and crept inside the hallway where blue and green panes surrounding a panel of birds and acanthus leaves threw coloured light over the tiles. It was a watery cavern cut off from the sounds of the street outside, in which the children moved stealthily like goldfish in a green bowl. Their fingers found each other's thighs, hidden lips and creases; touched, pressed and stroked, dared to stray over the white flesh into crevices and over hard mounds, as the scent of the forlorn tangled garden crept in through the crack of the door.

Now the secret knowledge was passed on while Mona was out. Betty leaned back over the plush sofa and pulled down her clothes. The boys giggled, fumbled with their flies and pulled girls' hands towards them, while Matt lolled shyly on the pegged rug watching.

"Thar'll soon learn," said Norman and sang into his ear.
"Apples are red, and nuts are brown,
Petticoats up and trousers down,
When cocks are up they're ready for sucking,
Girls lying down are ready for fucking."

Chapter XIV

LOCKED IN ICE

On a night of pin-prick stars and full moon when the village was washed by white streaming light and owls swept hunting from the woods, there was a brief lull in the hurly-burly. Norman, Reuben and Matt whistled each other up and met on the waste-ground to climb the gantry into the deserted sorting shed. They looked out through the slits in the corrugated walls over the railway yards ahead and to the rows of houses which ran up the hill beyond, their slate roofs washed in silver.

The black velvet sky merged into the coal tips and machine shops, erasing hard edges and outlines, and the valley lay still as the interior of a great vaulted cathedral. The boys leaned out contemplating this dark splendour, their voices hushed and echoing under the iron roof like plainsong, while the railway lines rippled and glittered beneath them and steam rose from the wheel-house to climb directly into the sky in a white perpendicular column. They felt the night lift them and move them as they lay on their backs and floated towards the intense light, lost in the endless parabolas of the stars. In a kind of worship they sang out, their voices ringing loud in the dark sheds, clear and compelling as the cry of nightingales. It was the start of the winter solstice.

Snow came howling across from the moors and blew into six-foot drifts blocking the roads. Giant icicles hung from the telephone wires and the wind sang harshly through the pylons calling the village to surrender. Banked in on all sides, and with the surrounding hills frozen and dangerous, the traffic came to a halt and the small community was cut off from its neighbours.

Jess Bedford made a long wooden sledge and fixed to it stout runners which a mate had forged for him in the pit metal shop. With Matt and a gang of his friends he dragged it to the top of the hill where the main road led to town. The boys clambered on and rushed downward at breakneck speed. At the bottom a convoy of lorries and buses stood locked in the drifts while their drivers tried in vain to dig them out.

Jess found the local delivery van which had a load intended for Ma Bedford's shop. The boys hauled out the bags of potatoes, bread, groceries, and a side of bacon and piled it on the sledge while the men joked and drank from a flask of whisky, and then, shouting and snowballing, pulled it back up to the village.

Snow kept falling until the colliery tips were blurred into white mounds of upturned blancmange and children bellyflopped down Grassmoor Hill flattening themselves as they steered under the railings to glide over the frozen pond. Youths lit bonfires in the middle of the lanes and wearing borrowed pit helmets and their father's steel-capped boots, raced headlong downhill between lines of girls waving torches. On the way back up they seized hold of one or two grinning likely ones, and threw them squealing into the drifts, legs and arms thrashing in the powdery snow. When the school closed down a week early before the Christmas holidays the delighted children took to the hills from early morning. The sledging got more reckless as they piled up three or four at a time on great six-footer toboggans and charged down the slopes.

In the houses the fireguards were piled high with wet clothes, and boots were put to dry overnight in the ovens after the fires had been raked out. The women threw the ashes over the paths and swept and shovelled, but still the snow came drifting down and lay in thick fresh blankets. The passageway in Ma Bedford's shop dripped and oozed from the tramp of customer's feet. It was Matt's job to swill out and lay potato sacks underfoot, and then make tea for favoured old ladies in the back parlour where they could sit for a while and warm themselves.

On the last few evenings Ma Bedford and Matt got the shop and house ready for the festive season. He went into the wood and brought armfuls of fir, ivy and holly, carrying it proudly through the pit yard and home. His mam polished and cleaned, pinned up crepe paper on the shelves in the shop, and artfully turned the puddings and glistening boxes of crackers to catch the light. They put up streamers and tinsel in loops across the ceiling and a bunch of mistletoe in the hall. Matt tied the greenery in garlands around the kitchen walls while his mother, humming to herself, turned out the drawers, searched through the back corners of cupboards and shelves and gathered together combs, pencils, silk thread, rattles, whistles and marbles. She wrapped them all in red paper and dropped them into an empty biscuit box for a lucky dip for the children.

Old Hoskin came down from his bothy in the wood and stood shyly just inside the shop door.

"Ay up, mi 'owd lad." Ma Bedford greeted him. "Ah thought we'd see thee soon, 'as thar come for thi mince pie? Well ma duck, thee stop 'ere for a minute, and our lad ull get thi a plateful. 'Urry up Matt, and pour 'im a big glass o'whisky off t'sideboard."

Hoskin lived alone in a shack of boughs and bracken. He snared rabbits, kept goats and chickens and doctored himself on wild roots. There was little he needed; some tea, tobacco, an occasional bundle of old clothes and boots, so he only rarely walked down into the village, but he always called at Christmas to pay his respects.

Ma Bedford beamed as he sipped his whisky and devoured the mince pies. Afterwards, his eyes full of tears, he sang old country songs of the greenwood. His quavering voice rose and fell as he sang ancient carols in a dialect that came from far-away parts, and he laughed and danced crazily into the street outside where neighbours came to the door steps and watched the children caper after him as ne played old mummers' rituals, leaping over his stick and reciting in a high pitched monotone.

Ma Bedford gave him a bag of mint rock and a tin of tobacco and dropped five shillings in his pocket.

"One of nature's gentlemen," said Jess as they watched him shamble off to the pub, and Matt thought he looked exactly like one of the shepherds on the cards hanging from the mantlepiece in the parlour.

On Christmas Eve, when the landlord shut his door, the men went carolling round the houses. They stood outside Ma Bedford's and sang the wassailing and the Derby Ram, stamping and laughing when they forgot the words. Matt crept down and hid under the table some time after they had been let in and he judged that they would all be mellow enough.

A young miner pulled him out and he was thrown around high from hand to hand. They made him stand on the table and demanded a solo, and fell silent as the boy began.

"Thar ought to be in t'choir, lad. Thar just like a bloody throstle, what a bloody grand voice," one yelled when he finished.

"Thar reight," beamed Jess Bedford, "'e's started 'is lessons already, asn't thar, ma duck, once a week in town, an 'e's going in t'Festival in Sheffield soon, then 'e'll show thee." They fetched the young singer on Boxing Day to the Miner's Welfare where he sang his heart out for an hour and got five pounds when they passed the hat round, and his mother, who had never before entered the place, sat in a corner listening proudly.

Matt was soon recruited to a village concert party which performed on rickety stages of trestle tables in schools and halls around the area. Dressed in a borrowed cassock and surplice, he sang sacred songs high and clear in a pure treble voice, glancing for his cues to the lady accompanist in the corner.

They gave a concert in the town Infirmary in a hall smelling of antiseptic and strong tea. Matt peered through the curtains and watched the matron giving directions as the old people were wheeled in and placed in rows, nodding, grey haired and vacant-eyed. The curtains parted and his terrified gaze wandered along the front row as the opening chords rang out. He saw knotted hands gripping the arms of wheelchairs, yellowed skin and toothless gaping mouths. The first notes failed in his throat. The accompanist began again, hissing the opening words of the song, but again Matt failed to begin. An old man banged on the table with his tea mug and called out, "Go on, laddie, we shanna eat thee up. Don't be shy, lad. Shall ah start thee off?"

He began the familiar song, and Matt joined in. He grew more confident, and by the end of the song his voice rang round the hall.

The matron found him weeping bitterly in a back room. "Come and get your tea, love. Ther's a nice tea waiting for your troupe when you've done. And don't worry. They're lovely, you know, but they've had their day. You shouldn't cry, your day's to come yet."

Soon it was the day of the annual village outing to the pantomime. The children fidgetted and fretted all afternoon until they were combed, scrubbed and ready, and allowed to run up the hill and wait for the charabancs. This year it was the Theatre Royal at Nottingham, not too far away, so there was plenty of time for everyone to have a good tea first and not to get in a fluster. The women donned their best hats and head scarves, powdered their noses and put neatly folded lace handkerchiefs in their polished handbags. They met in little groups at the street-ends feeling somewhat stiff and uncomfortable in their unaccustomed finery, and walked up arm in arm to the waiting coaches.

The men strolled clean shaven and silk-mufflered into the tap room and ordered a few rounds, exasperating the rest of the party as the time drew near to leave.

"It's allus same," complained Mrs. Bates. "It don't matter where yer goin', men is allus same. Yer get yerself ready, yer all primed to go, all keyed up, then what they do? Nip off boozin, they can't live wi'out it. Booze, booze, an' it's us what 'ave to 'ang about an' wait."

"Ay an' we'll be waiting some more, Gladys, if thar asks me," answered Ma Lawton.

"Look at 'em shovin' t'crates in t'glory 'ole at t'back. Bye me, there'll be some singin' tonight on t'way 'ome. Come on, shake yourselves, lads," Mrs. Bedford shouted through the gap after she had wound the window down. "Come on, 'urry up, yer buggers."

She settled herself down in her seat and opened a large box of chocolates. "Eh May, it's not often we 'ave a fuddle like this, is it duck?" she said, squeezing the girl around her shoulders, "ah'm lookin' forward to this, it'll be a rare treat."

The charabancs rumbled off in the soft evening light, past the neighbouring colliery villages towards the Nottinghamshire/Derbyshire border and on through Sherwood Forest. In an hour and a half the party were installed in the red-velvet grand circle of the old theatre. They chattered excitedly and passed round their sweets as the orchestra tuned up and began the overture. There was much to admire in the gilt decorations and the sparkling chandeliers, the tiers of boxes delicately overlaid in curving plasterwork and the huge swag of gold-fringed curtain which soon rose to expectant applause, revealing a ravishing scene.

Black and white timbered cottages flanked the stage, with banks of hollyhocks and roses climbing as high as the painted thatched roofs. There was an old-fashioned well in the foreground around which a band of young rustics danced and sang the opening chorus, and behind, a cleverly arranged perspective revealed a vista of a forest surmounted by the pinnacles of a turreted castle. The stage was bathed in a brilliant light from the smoking lamps overhead and the row of footlights which was fitted with garishly coloured celluloid filters.

The orange-wigged dame entered to cheers and thunderous applause, and the principal boy pranced on, slapping her generous thighs. She wore long boots and a jacket with brass buttons, fishnet tights and a three cornered hat cockaded with a white ostrich feather which nodded up and down as she strutted the width of the stage performing a series of amazing high kicks.

The men cheered her, and everyone joined in the chorus of her hunting song as she cracked her whip and challenged the villain.

The principal girl was a delight in her pale-blue rags and long blond wig. She sang sentimentally as she waltzed with her broom over the stone-flagged kitchen floor and cried heartbreakingly when the step-sisters flounced off to the ball.

There was a grand transformation scene which caused gasps of admiration and a comedy routine performed by a troupe of midgets in a wonderful bakehouse scene, who shot in and out of the ovens in a series of astonishing acrobatic tricks and landed, to the audience's delight, upside down in tubs of dough.

In the second half, during the aerial ballet, a plump fairy flew on her wire from the footlights and landed tip-toe on the edge of the circle. Then more fairies were flown in, their gauzy sequined wings dazzling in the spotlights, and were suspended in a ravishing tableau high in the dome of the auditorium.

As the play proceeded, a pattern emerged between the heroes and the villains, between the comedy and the sentiment. The comedians would convulse the audience with their antics and local humour, and then the moustached baron would enter in a flash of green lightning to be met by boos and hisses which rang the rafters. Minor acts were played out before a drop curtain and the attention of the audience would wander as they waited for the next compelling spectacle.

The quality of this expert arrangement sustained them to the very end when the curtain rose on the final scene and the house thrilled in anticipation. Down the gilded staircase came an entire court. The ladies were arrayed in crinolines of silver and lace, with tall white wigs on their heads and curls framing their delicately rouged cheeks, their fans fluttering as they danced a stately minuet.

Standing in decorous lines, the men, dressed in satin breeches and hose, bowed gravely and kissed the ladies' hands. There was a general curtsey, the lines parted like waves, and the triumphant pair of lovers ran towards each other and embraced. The audience rose as one man and roared its approval.

After that outing, and the annual tea for wives in the Working Men's

Club, the rest of the winter seemed interminable. The first fresh snow turned to rutted ice and then to slush which stayed for weeks, bringing the sledging and games to an end.

Work resumed in the schoolrooms which were now gloomy from the leaden sky outside, and chilly in spite of the hissing radiators.

In the Spring a new headmaster, Mr. Evans arrived and went round the school on a tour of inspection. He clearly did not approve of this rural scholastic backwater and rigorously set about a wholesale series of major changes.

Young and energetic, his manner was punctilliously polite, almost brusque, and at first the older teachers regarded him with suspicion. But his radical Welsh determination to upgrade the backward village school began to fire the imagination of the staff and the brighter pupils.

He brought books to start a library, drew up lists of required reading for the older classes, set homework, and more unconventional still, entered a few pupils in the examinations for the Grammar School in the nearby town.

Matt began to respond to this new stimulus. He found great pleasure in the books and read fervidly while the radio played in the evening and late at night by candlelight in bed.

Ma Bedford and Jess watched a change come over the boy. He seemed to draw into himself, curled up in the armchair poring over the new work. They smiled to each other as they sat by the fire and remembered their own childhood.

COMPOSITION – MATT BEDFORD
A Day in the Holidays

We all went to see the pit ponies being brought up for their annual holiday. They can only bring them up two at a time because there is not much room in the cage. Also, they have to wind it up very slowly so that they do not panic. The ponies have been down the pit a year and they are frightened by the light, so they have to wear blinkers. It is very hard for the keeper to control them when they are brought out of the cage into the light because the blinkers do not keep out all the light so they buck and kick. When they are all up the men drive them through the yard. They went mad and we all had to stand back or get kicked.

The ponies are allowed to graze in the dumble fields behind the quarry for a month and then they have to go down the pit to work again. Mr. Jackson says it is not cruel, because the colliers are very fond of the ponies and give them any snap they have left over. Also they take them apples. When they have settled down a bit and you can stroke them you can ride them bareback. Last year Joe Yates broke a leg trying. I should love to try if I can find a friendly one and ride it fast across the dumbles holding on to its mane. Mr. Jackson has a Bible which was given to his father for 25 years service down the mine as a pony keeper. It is written on inside with his name and the dates.

Chapter XV
JUMPING THE BROOMSTICK

Daisy Bedford, nee Randall, was one of thirteen raised in a small terraced cottage in Chesterfield. The little house, in a gas-lit alley by the canal, was scrubbed and worn, but teeming with warm affection as the children were whelped at random by the God fearing parents.

The matriarch of the family was a large comfortable woman, dignified in long black skirts and floury smooth of complexion, who ruled her household with gentle reproof, only occasionally goaded into stern and temporarily unforgiving silence, when her straight back and pained stare would carve misery into her repentant brood.

The father had a lively spirit, wiry and tenacious as the Jack Russells he kept in the back yard. He rose before dawn and worked till late evening, labouring, portering, gardening, and anxious to put his hand to anything that would bring in a few shillings to support his clamorous family. The children went out early with him. They carried crates in the market, fetched beer and swilled out for the shopkeepers. After school and tea they would run back into town to try and be first for the evening work and a few more coppers. Under the kerosene lamps the bargaining went on at the stalls until late at night, while the children did a second shift.

There were vegetables to be washed and trimmed, horses to be fed and watered, and great bales of cloth to be heaved on to wagons. But afterwards there were the pickings of discarded fruit and cabbage leaves, perhaps a lump of suet from a butcher, or scraps of batter and cold chips from the fish frier.

The back range in the cottage was kept alight in coal sweepings from the goods yard, brought home on a soap-box; and the mother kept a large china panshion simmering in the oven for the bones and trimmings retrieved by the children.

They fed on this daily with her own bread and wedges of Yorkshire pudding smothered in treacle. The boys grew up strong and hale and went off to war, leaving the girls in the Free School.

When Daisy was thirteen she started at the Mill. She learned to sort the differing grades of cotton, then went on to the carding shops and the vast roar of machinery. There the girls communicated in sign language to overcome the deafening pound of the engines and looms, and sang out brashly against the din. They raced out from their captivity at dinner-time to eat their snap and bathe naked in the mill stream which came straight off the moor.

Daisy brushed her hair with a piece of folded silk till it shone raven as a coal seam and dazzled the men. She grew tall and bright-eyed, proud of her good looks, and practised the teasing ways of the other mill lasses, strolling casually past the apprentices with knowing looks, winks and challenging banter.

At sixteen, proud of her contribution to the family purse, she had blossomed into a rare oval-faced beauty, thrifty and clever with a needle. She bought shantung in the market and made blouses embroidered with penny threads, polished her patent strapped shoes and paraded in the town promenade on Saturday nights elegant in a straw hat trimmed with ribbon and artificial flowers.

When her brothers came back after the war, she was courting a lad from a croft at Holymoorside who took her to the dances at the Corn Exchange. An elderly M.C., took them through the intricacies of the Violet Tango and the Quadrilles, breathless evenings of waltzes and Barn Dances, red-faced Jess Bedford hot and perspiring in his stiff collar and white gloves, and Daisy flushed with the whirling.

The lads had escaped luckily, apart from the eldest one who lost a leg at Ypres.

They adored their newly grown-up sister and were immensely pleased that she had managed to keep the house and the ageing parents comfortable through the long war.

She was proud of her raw boned Jess who was going to leave the farm and get a job in the pits. She had saved money in the old teapot on the dresser and sewn a bottom drawerful of voile and crepe finery. Her mother gave her a wash tub, a poncher and some old pans which Jess piled with their straw boxes on a dray.

They came to this colliery house in the village perched on a hill where there was always a wind from the facing moors. It flew down into the valley across the belching smoke stacks, but the house was cosy on the weekly coal allowance, the brick floor soon shone, and the bits of shabby furniture lasted them for a while as they worked and prospered.

Through the strikes and the following miserable slump when men were laid off from the mines, mooning forlornly in their pigeon coops, they forged a precarious life together. Jess found new work on the railway as a ganger, revelling in the open air life after the dust and dark of the underground galleries. He would come home late after a long shift on the line, and work well into the night preparing the shop which Daisy was to run in the converted front parlour. After fitting shelves, cupboards and a counter, they set about acquiring some stock. At first it was a meagre display of the few basic essentials that they and the hard pressed villagers could afford, but when the men went back to work the wives could pay off a few shillings from the slate. The shop's credit grew, and the travelling salesmen, impressed with Daisy's careful ordering and prompt settling, pressed more goods on her till the little shop was bursting.

There were hams and bacon hung from the ceiling, scuttles, rat traps and feather dusters; shelves of horse liniment, camphor, wintergreen and liver pills in jars. Drawers were crammed with blacklead, rubstone and dolly blue, bootlaces, pegs and clout nails. On Wednesdays there was potted meat for tea, on Thursdays a van brought pork pies, chitterlings, black puddings and brawn. On Fridays fish was sent from the town market, and tripe on Saturdays.

In the early mornings the miners came in for plug tobacco to chew on the shift and called in on their way home for packets of Woodbine. The women used the yard running down to the shop for a meeting place, glad of some distraction from the endless washing, scrubbing and baking in their crowded kitchens.

Daisy slaved for perfection in her bright parlour. She gloried in her strength and good fortune with these strangers who had welcomed her into their midst. When her son arrived her happiness was even more complete. The villagers, recognising this, gave her a title. They called her Ma Bedford.

"Yes," she thought to herself, watching the boy at work on his books, "this lad of mine won't go down no dark hole in the ground, clawing at rock when there's a bad fall or choking in the gas. He'll wear a clean shirt and a tidy pressed suit and marry a nice young lass who'll make him a good wife like that May Barlow."

COMPOSITION – MATT BEDFORD
An outing to the seaside.

The choir and Sunday School outing to Skegness was on Whit Monday. We had to be up very early for the coaches. It was still dark when we took off but the weather got better as we went along. The sun came out as we went through Sherwood Forest so we cheered up. The land is very flat when you get into Lincolnshire. We saw dykes everywhere and a windmill. There are not many houses and the roads are narrow. When the coaches stopped we could smell the sea. We got there about ten o'clock. It was very cold at first and we all had to keep our coats on. The sea at Skegness is very rough so we could only paddle at the edge. There was a prize for the best sand castle and everybody had a go. It was won by Maureen Ashley and Jennifer Ralston. I had my picture taken with Ernest Hewitt on a motor bike. There was also a monkey you could hold. We had our dinners in a cafe where we could sit and watch the sea. Afterwards we went to the funfair and went on the big dipper and the helter skelter.

Joyce Lawton went swimming in the sea and we all had to wait for her while she got dry. Mrs. Lawton was angry with her for going in when it was rough, but she got on alright. We had our teas in Newark on the way back and coming home afterwards we all sang. Everybody wished it had been warmer but we had a very good day.

Chapter XVI

SECRET AFTERNOON

The class streamed out over the asphalt yard in a tumult. They climbed up on the bottom playground wall and sat there for a while in the sun. The engines shunted up and down the line and the boys called out to the drivers, sliding and slithering about on the shiny coping stones which were worn to a high polish by legs and bottoms.

"If yer want, yer can come to t'guard's van," one said to Matt, sniffing into his jersey sleeve.

"What guard's van?"

"That one at t'end o' t' siding."

He pointed along the track leading towards the first railway bridge over the lane which curved into the wood.

"What do yer go there for?"

"It's our camp," exclaimed Reuben, "and nobody else goes there. It's bin empty and just left there, and now it's ours."

"We'd better go and get t'things, Reub," said Tom, winking at his friend. "Thee stop 'ere. We'll come back for thee."

They slurped off the wall, scattering into the village streets like magpies, leaving Matt alone on the wall. He whistled as he sat there swinging his legs in circles. The bottom halves went round like the Red Emmas in the playground, he thought, two going in opposite directions. The wall was warm and he felt quite contented waiting there for these older boys who had suddenly taken him up.

A young pit lad was crossing the colliery yard on the other side of the railway tracks. He stepped by the big elderberry tree and plucked a flower to stick in his cap. Matt watched him stand and stare at the sun, breathing the fresh air down deep in his lungs.

Joe Yates had just got out of short trousers and left school to work as an apprentice on the pit top. Cock of all the boys and now one of the men, with five of his older brothers working within shouting distance so they could watch out for him and save him from many a thick ear, he swaggered in his new job and brought home his wages for his mam's teapot.

Everyone in the village knew what they were up to, those boys. Whippets and ferrets in the coal-house, first out for blue-stalks and black-berries, good at scrumping, they could come back with a sack of ripe pears after an evening's rabbiting, sometimes with a chicken under a jacket.

Mrs. Yates championed her ruffian sons and only thrashed them if they fought in the parlour and broke her precious ornaments.

Joe eased himself from one foot to the other, blinking in the strong yellow light and pulling his thin body together after the pounding it had been given on the tub caterpillar all the morning shift. His job was to throw short lengths of hardwood at the tub wheels to lock a convoy as it crashed down the gradient. You had to throw it properly, they said, you had to be a boy that could smash a pigeon's nest with one stone, or pulverise a frog on the other side of a pond, because if you missed, and the prop failed to lock the wheel, half a dozen tubs full of muck could crash over the top and break a man's legs. Joe had a pride in his work and the burly day-men felt confident with him, but he did not realise that he had been bred and trained for the work from birth like one of his own ferrets.

With his eyes glowing in his bony black face he suddenly caught sight of Matt, and putting two fingers to his lips, whistled across the waste-ground.

"Ay-up, thee. Wheer are they then? Ah'm waitin."

"They shan't be long, they'll be back in a minute," called Matt.

"Ah'm not 'angin' about for anymun. Does thar want to come wi' me, young un?" enquired Joe, moving towards Matt through the clumps of willow-herb at the top of the embankment.

The boy slid off the wall and vaulted over the fence. They walked along the railway track, one foot in front of the other, balancing with their arms outstretched, to the end of the siding.

Joe offered no more conversation, so Matt followed in silence concentrating his attention on the glossy line, not wanting to speak for fear of spoiling things. Him a working lad, and the two of them walking out together for the afternoon; he smiled to himself.

Soon they got to the abandoned van. It was dark and dull, even on such a bright day, standing weightily on its rusted wheels, the only relief in colour being the chalkings over the wooden sides which recorded its past journeys around the Eastern Region as far as Lincoln and Grimsby and down to Kettering in the south.

They stepped up on to the iron foot plate and climbed the ladder. A half-door with an engraved brass latch stood ajar, flanked by a pair of blackened oil lamps. They pushed it open and went inside. Joe sat down, grinning proudly, and let Matt wander about. He inspected a pile of dingy ledgers, a box of candles, and a cupboard in which he found a guard's cap, a faded great coat, a broken pipe, some empty tobacco tins which still smelled sweetly, and an old tattered Punch magazine. There was a small folding table and a stove, and down both sides, seats covered in floral plush with the flowers barely visible under a patina of grease and grime.

The air was hot and still, reeking of paraffin oil.

Matt began to feel flustered by the close atmosphere and sat down by the small window, clearing a circle with the back of his hand to look out.

Joe moved over to the opposite corner, dropping down on a bench, and sprawled his legs over the rail of the stove. He loosened the bits of string tied around his trousers beneath the knee and unwound the rag from his throat.

Matt turned imperceptibly towards him, watching from under lowered eyelids as Joe ran his tongue over his downy upper lip and closed his eyes, yawning.

Faint sounds came from the distant yards and fields. The old van creaked slightly as the sun stirred its timbers and insects trembled at the window in the warmth.

Matt shifted his feet uneasily and thought of trying to slip away, but Joe eased himself forward and suddenly a racking tremor shook his whip-lash body. Specks of ebony-coloured grit flew from his hair and his clothes as the movement brought him to his feet. For a moment he steadied himself by the fireguard, then coughed harshly, bringing up the black dust from his lungs in painful bursts. There was a long pause during which the sounds from outside seemed to take over the hot interior of the cabin again, and Joe seemed quite unaware of the boy sitting quietly in the corner. But then he shifted, took a piece of chalk from a shelf, marched to the centre of the floor and marked it with a cross. He stepped back and spat accurately in the centre of it. Grinning wickedly at Matt he ground the phlegm with his boot. Fumbling in a waistcoat pocket Joe then brought out a Woodbine from a screwed up packet, lit up, and passed it on. Matt sucked at the cigarette, choking, while tears sprang to his eyes.

"Try agen, it's alreight when you get used to it, kid. Ah'll show thee 'ow to blow it down yer nose. Gi'e it 'ere," said Joe, taking back the fag. The blue smoke circled gracefully as he fished his open mouth about trying to suck it back in. He blew out with a gasp, trying to force the smoke through his nostrils. Like a bullock, thought Matt, on a cold winter morning snorting out steam.

"Nah thee try." Choking on the acrid taste, Matt did reluctantly as he was told, but his ordeal came to an end when the door burst open and half a dozen boys clambered inside the cabin.

"Ere, save us a drag. Ah gid thi a fag yesterday, does thar remember? Thar owes me one," exclaimed Reuben. "Ah looked in mi feyther's coat fer 'is dogs but ah think 'e knows ah've bin pinchin'. 'E's got right bloody cheeky and smoked the buggers up."

The tousled red haired Tom squashed himself into one of the benches.

"Shove up and mek room for a little un then." They passed the cigarette from hand to hand around the group.

"'Ere, look what thar's done, thar's made a real piss-corner aht of it."

"Shut thi gob an' gie it 'ere."

Feeling even more shy with the new arrivals, Matt sidled across the van and went out on to the verandah at the back for a while.

"Come back in 'ere kid, thar'll be seen, an' some soddin' nosey parker ull tell on us," Joe called after him.

Inside a boy was raking out the iron stove with a poker, laying the good ashes aside. He laid paper and sticks and soon there was a blazing fire adding to the already stifling heat. They all took their snap from their pockets and tossed it into a cardboard box which they placed on the folding table. Joe took the first lion's share and then the others dived in. They had raided their mams' pantries and brought doorstopper chunks of bread and dripping, bacon rinds, cold potatoes and cocoa and sugar mixed in twists of paper, all of which they ate voraciously till the last crumb was gone and they felt reasonably satisfied.

"Come on, Joe," yelled Reuben, when the picnic was finished. "Let's 'ave a look at it."

The boys gathered in a tight circle around Joe, squatting on their haunches like miners. Joe, slumped in the greasy folding chair, smiled as he wiped his mouth with the back of his hand. After a moment the other hand travelled down his body, scratching at his chest through his thin shirt. He fingered the brass buckle of his belt and slowly opened his buttons.

The boys gasped. "Eeh, it's black just like thee".

"What would yer expect, yer silly twats, when ah've bin in t'muck all day," he countered', "it gets everywhere, dun't it; but see 'ere." He slowly pulled his foreskin back, bending down like the others to admire the pink glistening tip which was the only part of his body which had escaped the all penetrating dust. Tom sniggered. "Go on then Joe, show us, see 'ow quick thar can do it."

"All reight then," he leered, "are yer watchin'?" His grimy fingers sped up and down, a wolfish grin on his face, and a trickle of perspiration made lines through the dust on his forehead. He stood up in the middle of the circle. Matt watched, fascinated, and the rest of the boys counted out loud together, stamping their feet on the floor and banging with their fists on the wooden walls.

Suddenly Joe let out a gasp and shuddered. The boys cheered as the milky juice spurted out, startling white against his blackened hands, as far as the burning stove.

In silence they watched it sizzle, bubbling in droplets and hissing till it was gone, leaving an acrid odour in the hot air. Joe casually wiped his hand on his trouser leg, rubbing a few traces into the crystalline dust and lit up another cigarette.

They dawdled there for a while in the late afternoon until they were bored with hanging about. As they got up to go, Tom kicked Matt up the backside and said off-handedly, "When we whistle up ternight, thar can come if thar wants to. We're goin' tormentin'."

Chapter XVII

NIGHT GAMES

When the call came Matt bolted his supper and washed it down hurriedly at the kitchen tap. He pulled on a balaclava and raced out of the back door before his ma could ask him what his intentions were.

The gang were meeting up by the weather-beaten old beech tree in the allotments. They had to sneak over the fence and crawl on their bellies between the rows of bean poles to avoid being seen by the few men who were still out working on their plots. Joe stuffed his pockets with anything edible he could find on the way and sat with his back to the tree trunk nibbling his loot.

One by one the gardeners picked their way homewards in the gathering darkness. Joe, whispering in Tom's ear, pointed out a shed nearby. Tom edged towards it and cautiously lifted the sneck of the door. A few minutes later he came back with a length of rope which Joe threw over the lowest branch of the great tree to help them climb up.

Matt, perched up above, watched curiously as Reuben, who had stayed down below, threw a large reel of thread which Joe caught and speared with a long nail through the bobbin. Reuben then crept stealthily towards the fence, holding the end of the thread which Joe payed out on the improvised spindle. Peering through the dark they watched him climb over and then disappear in an alley which led towards Granny Wainwright's backyard. Suddenly he was silently vaulting and racing back towards the tree. He shinned up and hauled the rope after him.

They sat impassively in the tree watching the house. A light came on in a window. "'Ere she comes, the rotten cow," Joe hissed, "She'll be shittin' 'er knickers afore long when ah've done wi' 'er, just you wait." He held the bobbin up, moving it rythmically forwards and backwards a few inches, playing the thread. After a few moments they saw Granny Wainwright open the door a few inches. The boys sniggered as she poked her head out and looked about the yard.

Joe held his hand still. "She'll never see it in t'dark," he spluttered. "Ah bet she thought it were some kid tappin' what's run away."

They watched her turn and close the door. "Gi'e it another go," urged Reuben.

"Nay, not yet, let 'er get settled in t'front o' t'fire afore we 'ave another bash. Then it's my turn," said Norman, taking the bobbin from Joe.

In a while he began, moving the bobbin carefully. The door opened wider this time. Granny Wainwright appeared in a shaft of light which spilled across the yard. "Who is it," they heard her call, "Who's knockin'?" She moved cautiously across the cobbles, peering down the alley. "If it's you buggers again, tormentin', yer can clear off," she squawked in her frail voice before hobbling back and slamming the door.

"What is it yer doin'," asked Matt, "why does she keep comin' to t'door like that?"

The other boys swivelled round and gawped in amazement. Joe explained.

"Thar daft arn't thar. Sithee, there's a washer fastened on t'line, and Reuben stuck a drawin' pin at t'end o' t'cotton on 'er winder frame. When yer shift t'cotton like this it makes t'washer tap on t'winder and she thinks there's somebody outside."

"Or ghosts", Reuben laughed, "she'll think she's 'aunted afore we've done wi' 'er." He snatched the bobbin and played it faster. The back door opened again. This time Granny Wainwright rushed out like a termagent, brandishing a carving knife.

"Ah'll cut yer bloody 'and off if ah catch yer, yer little swine," she screamed, "just come 'ere and show yer faces if yer durst, what yer doing comin' tormentin' me for?" The boys watched in paroxysms of glee as she tore fiendishly down the alley and round the back of the middens. She gave a fearsome shriek as she crashed into the dustbins, then came back into view cursing and gesticulating wildly.

A penetrating wail came from inside the house, at which she turned and flew back inside.

"What was that?" gasped Matt, terrified.

"That's Dorothy, chained to 'er bed. She's bin there locked up forty years they say, she's got long white hair hangin' down 'er back and she never comes out. She's a lunatic," Joe said in a rush.

"No she's not," Tom chimed in, "my mother says 'ow she 'ad a babby when she wor a lass about thirteen an' 'er mother locked 'er up so she couldn't do it again. Anyway, she's theer, and nobody ever sees 'er, so she must be locked up or chained, and they all say 'ow t'owd lass 'as bin seen carryin' t'slop bucket across t'yard in t'middle o' t'night. And that proves she's theer. That's 'er shit what she's carryin."

The downstairs light went out and a glow came from upstairs as an oil lamp was carried past the landing window. Joe beckoned Matt nearer along the branch.

"Nar, young un, ah'll tell thi what thar's got ter do if thar wants ter be in t'gang. She's got an old 'armonium in t'yard, covered in tarpaulin. It were ter wide ter get in t'door and she wain't get rid of it. When she's gone ter bed, thee go and climb up t'drainpipe and fix t'washer on t'bedroom winder. Then when she oppens up we'll pump up t'organ and gi'e it a right bleedin' blow."

In a fit of snorts and giggles he scrambled down the rope with the others following. Like footpads they advanced towards the house, winding up the spare thread as they went. Tom tiptoed through the alley, pushing Matt before him, and gave him a leg up the drainpipe. Matt fixed the drawing pin on the upstairs window frame as directed and then dropped down silently. Meantime the other boys were stealthily sliding the tarpaulin off the old harmonium. It sat incongruously on the cobbled yard, with its heavy mahogany carving and pleated silk mildewed from the damp. The stops and pedals were stiff, but the gang managed to pump some air into the bellows which creaked and wheezed. Joe gave a signal for them to wait a while. He began the tapping, jiggling the bobbin slowly at first, then faster. As the bedroom light came on, Tom pumped furiously at the pedals. When Granny Wainwright threw up the window, hoarsely screaming her wild abuse into the dark, the entire gang descended on the ivory keys, making a huge crescendo of discordant sound which blasted the enclosed yard.

In their delirium they did not notice Granny Wainwright dashing away from the window. They played on in frantic abandon till she came back screaming holy murder with a chamber-pot and emptied the stinking contents all over them.

The gang wrought sweet revenge on the old harridan a few weeks later. Extra reinforcements were needed, so some more green boys were invited along to the cabin to hear Joe unfold his elaborate plans.

The come-uppance was arranged for a particular night when an away team had a date to play darts at the Welfare up the hill. There was to be a supper and a concert afterwards, a popular attraction which would draw a large crowd, leaving the village fairly quiet.

The night was chill and foggy. Wreaths of smoke drooped down from the chimneys and barely stirred in the cutting. Joe, leading his mongrel on a string, summoned the boys away from the cabin and led them along the line to a point just below Granny Wainwright's cottage. They lay in the long damp grass, listening to doors slamming and neighbours calling to each other as they picked their way with torches up the hill. "They'll be pissed as farts afore long," Reuben muttered. "If we get on wi' it, we'll 'ave done by t'time us dads get back."

"'Ang on a bit, there's got to be dead quiet. We're not startin' yet," Joe said with an air of finality. He lit a fag and graciously passed it around. He could imagine that he was on some secret manoeuvre, involving spies and enemy agents, an adventure straight out of Boys Own Paper.

"Come on, let's move forward," he commanded, after a decent pause. When they reached the alley, they took off their shoes before they loped towards Granny Wainwright's yard and scaled the fence. Tom and Norman placed the sacks they had been carrying near the outhouse wall while the others deftly began. A pair of clothes props were balanced between the gutter of the outhouse and the top of the fence opposite.

Then a dustbin full of rubbish was placed delicately on the props, flanked by a dozen beer bottles they had brought in a crate. They tied one end of a rope to the kitchen door handle and the other to one of the clothes props, and when they were satisfied with the arrangements, opened up the sacks and shared out the items for dressing-up.

There were old sheets and flour sacks with holes cut out for eyes, false noses, a battered trilby and orange peel cut into monstrous teeth. Reuben sported a voluminous nightgown and his mother's turban, and stood poised with a couple of saucepan lids. Norman had brought a mouth organ and a whistle and Matt wore a red indian suit complete with feather head-dress. Soon they were ready, balanced on the roofs of the wash house and the privy, the dog sitting obediently while Joe tied a string of tin cans to his tail. Then suddenly they began their caterwauling and banging, jumping up and down in their outlandish outfits.

Granny Wainwright catapulted from her rocking chair towards the door. As she opened it the rope pulled at the clothes prop and the dustbin and bottles came crashing down. The dog ran amok with the rattling tin cans and Norman shook out a cascade of feathers from an old bolster.

The old lady fought her way in panic through the din towards the refuge of the privy. It was a great mistake. The whooping boys in seconds had a rope through the handle and tied it to the knob of the coalhouse, very securely.

It was a great treat for half the village later, when the Welfare emptied after the darts, to witness the release of the closeted mother by the captive daughter.

Dorothy ran like a ghost across the cindered yard making strange whimpering, mewing sounds like a seagull, silver hair long enough for her to sit on streaming out behind her in the wind. In the moonlight her skin, bleached from years of incarceration, was the same colour as her ragged calico nightgown and the froth on her lips. As she tore at the knots in the rope with her finger nails, curved and long as parrot's claws, she mouthed a string of obscenities at the chortling crowd, her bare feet beating a frenzied dance into the hard ground. The onlookers were hushed when Granny finally stepped out, smoothing her skirts, for indeed the terrifying episode had caught her short. The old lady, with her arm around her liberator, made towards her back door with as much dignity as she could muster before turning with a grimace and a violent shake of her diminutive fist.

"Well, she can't 'ave bin chained up like wot folks say," said one bystander, "or else she wouldn't 'ave bin able ter get out an' stop these little bleeders tormentin' 'er old mother."

"Oh, ah doan't know," said Mrs. Pearson, her thick fingers covered in pastry from a meat pie she had just run from preparing, "Ah expect cos it was a cold night t'old bitch let Dotty come down for a bit ter warm 'er bum on t'fireguard. Perishin' cold, in't it?"

"Did yer see 'er moustache?" asked Mrs. Lake, "fair thick and brown, just like our Jack's. Funny on a woman, that."

"Don't be daft, that were t'cocoa, she'd just bin 'avin' a mug, yer could see it were still wet," Mona scoffed. "Talk about cocoa, ah could do wi' a nip o' somethin' meself, a bit stronger than cocoa though."

The crowd drifted off up the rows, laughing and calling goodnight. Peace reigned again for a short while the small gang of boys were led home by their respective fathers, ears tweaked between thumb and finger.

Granny Wainwright, letting out only a snatch of light from the curtain, peered out into the night with a toothless grin as the village suddenly rang out with the cries of boys getting their backsides tanned crimson from a few pit-belts being smartly applied.

Chapter XVIII

FLYING AWAY

Later on, in the early Spring, when the turbulently beautiful sky had calmed down and the lanes were pricked with the first eerie acid green shoots of hawthorn and glossy celandine, Matt would dawdle under the railway bridge waiting for May to come out of school, whittling the peel away from a twig of elderberry with his finger nail, or be idly occupied in rubbing dandelion flowers over his hands until they turned a brilliant stained saffron.

One Friday afternoon they lay on a bank high in the woods, where through a gap in the sycamores, they could see cranes, cables and wheel-houses dotted about the fields like so many miniatures on a toy railway set. Ten miles away the grey rocks of Stanedge, the first outcrop of Beeley Moor, thrust upwards away from the undulating skyline.

They lay propped on their elbows, eyes closed, listening to the stream rushing over rocks in a cleft just below them, while deep in the bank wild bees stirred towards the first warm afternoon of the year.

Matt searched among the fern roots for the entrance to the bees' nest, and teased away the winter debris of skeleton leaves from the hole. Placing his hand on it, he leaned over, pressing his ear tight to the cracks between his fingers. Soon, at the mouth of the tunnel, a bee crawled over the palm of his hand; holding his breath he lifted his head a few inches and spread his fingers wide. The great yellow bee crept out unsteadily, jabbing its pointed legs uncertainly while the warm sunshine played on the bank and the children watched in baited silence. A moment's stillness, then suddenly the bee was off, flying in a huge arc up and over as if signalled to some errand. As it flew away the children followed it until it was a speck and gone.

The wilderness of rock and heather in the distance lay waiting to be warmed and revived. Soon there would be an ocean of cottontail and ling for the myriads of wild insects to feed on, and the children, drunk with the smell of the damp earth where they were lying, vowed to race there. They wanted to fly over the sycamores and streams to the dark rocks of the moor, climbing wildly as hawks soar over open spaces.

"It can't be that far by us bikes," said May. "We could mek it bi dinner time, tek some snap, 'ave a picnic all afternoon and be back before dark."

"We'd 'ave ter check us tyres and tek a puncture kit. Them cart tracks up there is all chips and granite. Otherwise we'd be walkin' back," replied Matt.

"Ay and we could leave t'bikes under some bracken and go off for a long 'ike, then when we got back it'd be easy ridin' home, mostly down 'ill all t'way back."

May stood up quickly, brushing at her legs and skirt. The fine clay dust shimmered in the air as she tidied herself, shaking her long brown hair. While she was standing there in front of the boy, the wind gusted up the hillside stirring the alders. They both suddenly felt quite cold and shivered. She bent down giving him a hand to get up.

"Cum on, but don't tell anybody we're goin' that far, or else they waint let us." Matt pulled his jacket close round him and stayed quiet for a moment. The girl's tangled hair and her bright skin gave off an earthy scent from the bank where their bodies had bruised the celandine leaves. He wanted to take hold of her hand again, or to touch her face, but he lowered his head in silent panic.

"Beat yer ter t'bottom," cried May, darting like a suddenly startled rabbit through the undergrowth towards the stream and the stepping stone. She raced on, leaping over the massed tree roots, till she reached a stile which led to the track into the village. There she sat waiting for Matt, impatient because the last sun had gone and they still had a mile to walk home.

Chapter XIX
A HANDFUL OF LING

Matt came home breathless from an afternoon in the timber yard with the gang. They had managed to dodge the foreman and sneak in unnoticed. Once inside they could shout their heads off, re-enacting the cowboy films which spellbound them at the twopenny flicks on Saturdays without fear of being heard over the din of the colliery workings at full throttle.

The pine logs, stored for use as pit-props, were criss-crossed in layers, making piles as high as a man's head. These were arranged in neat avenues on a disused flattened tip near the quarry. Sometimes the pattern was broken where a few stacks had been accidentally misplaced. Good fortune for the village boys when four stacks were set corner to corner, enclosing a space which was invisible from the outside. By climbing over the top, they could drop down into a hidden resin-scented cave which could be roofed over with more timbers to provide an undetectable hide-out where precious possessions could be left quite safely until the next shoot-out.

The gang had put their claim on one particular den, marking it with chalk so faintly that a casual observer or a marauding boy from another gang would never notice it. Inside, an orange box held a valuable cache of home-made props. They had whittled boxwood into guns, tied up bundles of firewood with string for the essential dynamite, and filled sugar bags with sand to represent robbers' gold dust. There were useful bits of rag for face masks and bandannas and a cigar box filled with spent cartridges; various hand painted signs advertised thousands of dollars rewards for gangsters, dead or alive, and there were bottles of dandelion and burdock for the hard drinking in the saloon. The day was giddy with excitement and it was only the thought of their teas that broke up the stampede.

When Matt ran down the path, Mrs. Lakinshawe's tall frame was blocking the doorway in its usual angular fashion. She stood on one spindly leg, her lisle stockings hanging limply like so much unwanted skin. Her free foot was tucked out of sight up her pinny scratching somewhere behind her knee. She seemed lost in thought, polishing her glasses on her cardigan sleeve, but she brightened when she saw Matt.

"Ay up, duck, thar does look 'ot and bothered," and to Ma Bedford, "Well missus, it's your lad come 'ome for 'is tea, ah bet." "Evelyn," she shouted along the passage, "best start spreadin', young master's 'ere."

Matt ducked, trying to pass, but she trapped him between her arms, splaying her bony fingers wide on the counter top. "'Aven't seen thee, 'ave we," she said, mock menacingly. "Not for weeks, aren't we good enough for thee lately, ma lad? Ar Monica's pinin', don't know what ah'm goin' ter do wi' 'er." Jutting her jaw forward she winked grotesquely at Ma Bedford. The hair growing out of a mole on her chin quivered. "Ah don't know, 'e comes courtin' one minute, playin' ball on our 'ouse-end, readin' comics wi' 'er, gets 'er all flustered, then blow me 'e goes off and leaves 'er on 'er own. An' ah thowt they were sweethearts, didn't you, missus? What d'yer mek on 'im, eh?"

"Ooh, 'e's a proper lad is ar Matt, aren't thar luv, kisses them all, dusn't thar." Ma Bedford beamed at her son, "'e's got another fancy woman nar though, if ah'm not mistaken, Rose. 'E's tryin' ter mek your Monica jealous, that's what it is. Been out wi' 'er today 'as thar duck, eh?. What's 'er name, ah can't remember it for the life of me. Eh, Rose, what's that lass's name two doors away from you, that one 'e's stuck on, 'er what teks 'im bluebellin'?"

"Why, it's not 'er," Rose exploded, "not 'er is it? Damn me, nob'dy tells me nowt, ah never get's ter 'ear nuthin' o' t'tattle. Your lad courtin' that May Barlow, eh! Me an' ar Monica's 'ad ar necks put aht proper, a'n't we?"

Mrs. Lakinshawe jabbed a merciless finger in Matt's ribs.

"Well," she tittered, aren't thar a fawce one? Well nay mind, lad, if thar wants to come and see me thar'll be welcome, ah shan't 'old it against thee. Come and see t'new pups what t'grey'oun's 'ad eh?"

She pranced away on her stilt legs, wrapping her cardigan around her meccano frame of a body, leaving the crimson faced boy to sidle up the passage to the peace of the kitchen and tea with Evelyn.

Ma Bedford, fortified by cups of strong tea brought in by the girl, dealt with a good many customers before Mrs. Barlow and May came in for their order.

"Do me a favour, luv," she said to May, "put t'bolt on, ah've 'ad quite enough today, ah reckon ah'll make yoh two t'last uns. It's about seven isn't it? Are yer off now then, Ev?" she shouted, "Don't worry about nowt in theer, ah'll tidy up missen when ah've done in 'ere."

Then, turning to Mrs. Barlow, "Nah then, what can ah get yer, luv."

When Evelyn had gone out through the back Matt crept towards the passage door which stood ajar. The shop was quiet and darker now, and Ma Bedford was enjoying the special atmosphere of the end of the day. Her voice was low and confidential. May was lolling against the varnished wall, apparently taking little notice of the conversation. She turned her head and caught a glimpse of the boy in the nick of the door. When he shifted, a floor board creaked. He stood rooted to the spot, his heart pounding.

May was growing into a beautiful young girl, soft complexioned, with clearly defined cheekbones and abundant hair. In the light of the gas mantle her momentary impudent glance made her brown eyes shine and lips curl into a half smile.

At a different time, in another place she might have been a subject for the Pre-Raphaelite Brethren with her dark yearning looks and the sense in her bearing of burgeoning womanhood, tempered by a childish and grave calm.

There were prints of many a similar beauty in the local parlours. They languished through village Sunday teas when front rooms were opened up for visitors, draped on sofas or in fields of poppies, holding lilies and crowns of ivy; swans glided past them in tranquil rivers as they lay in harmonious groupings on the banks of meadowsweet. They looked down from their mahogany frames with great tenderness on the children huddled in corners, whose heads were bent over fraying copies of Elizabeth Barrett Browning, Enquire Within, or selections of Lord Alfred Tennyson. The pictures and the language of the limited reading material suffered the same moral purpose and a similar exquisite melancholy; a particularly affecting threnody of the inner self, aching, but rapturous.

An anguish ran through the boy. It had its origins in these divinely affected figures and the familiar sentiments in which the volumes were steeped, but at the same time it seemed to him to be coming directly from the wet battery attached to the fretted wireless set, undulating murmurs of Delius, a summer promenade concert by the Hallé in the Sheffield City Hall.

Hidden, trembling in the corner behind the heavy chenille curtain on its brass rail and the fractionally opened door, the boy experienced all the required pangs of ardour. His mother had no idea of the extra turmoil she was inducing when she suggested that May might like to step into the kitchen and have some tea with that bad lad of hers so that she could get down to a good chunter with Mrs. Barlow.

The talk in the shop ranged over Millie Jackson's misery and poor Reg, still drilling at Catterick, while the two children ate their bread and jam and squashed bananas in milk.

It was uplifting and sad at the same time for all of them.

By the time the flushed ladies had retired to the kitchen for a welcome pot of tea and a couple of biscuits, Matt had sensed that it would be a good time to ask if they could bike over to Beeley Moor the next day.

"That'll be nice," said Ma Bedford, "Yer can bring some 'eather back."

They got up while it was still dark. In the Bedfords' and the Barlows' houses, identical fireguards were folded away and the previous night's embers stirred into life to prepare breakfasts of scalding tea and bacon, with the bread dipped in the fat.

Heavily wrapped up against the chill, the children waved their goodbyes and met up by the bus stop on the main road.

Men were arriving for the first shift, treading through the village as quietly as they could manage in their steel-capped boots and clogs.

They heard the low wail of the siren announcing the first descent of the cage as they cycled off along the misty lanes. Cattle snorted over hedges and rabbits scuttled across their path. A fox eyed them warily from a bank of gorse before streaking away into a coppice, and a barn owl flew low across a field, startlingly white against the shadowy trees.

The colour of the sky ahead gradually changed as they sped through neighbouring villages, turning from slate blue to steel, and smoke from cottage chimneys rose and faltered in the still air.

It was suddenly cold and dark again when they rode between overhanging beeches in the valley, and when they began to climb again into the open country their clothes were damp from the dew.

They rested on a stone outcrop and looked back to the horizon which was streaked in pale salmon and ivory.

"Come on," said Matt, grabbing his bike, "We'll get to Stanedge in ten minutes if we get a move on. Wi' any luck we'll see t'sun come up from there."

They reached the great overhanging rocks and crashed through the brambles to climb up.

As the splendour began they were stricken with the same awe as the primitive hill people who had worshipped here. The massive grey rock, thrust out of the moor, lifted them towards the sun. They stood like eagles in an eyrie, lowlands undulating in folds and curves beneath them, and behind them the wild moor rising away to the north, crevasses and rushing water in secret gulleys. The first arc rose crimson, sending livid fingers of flame, staining the low clouds on the horizon. A wind stirred around the rocks, rusting the ling and the harebells, but the children stood motionless and watched the colour spread outwards. It was as crimson as the blood which was spilled in ancient sacrificial rites on these stones and dyed the bowl of the sky.

They followed the rise of the sun into denser cloud where it became partially obscured and the fiery glow subsided like a dying furnace. The rocks and the earth seemed to be waiting for the warmth, and the pools of rainwater which had collected on the smooth flat top of the stone shone again glassily.

Then, as if giant unseen winds swept across the sky, the cloud formations broke into long trailing strands of vapour and the sun burst through. They felt it suddenly on their faces, and saw the shadows of trees stab out to great distances in the fields below. There was a jangle of birds in the heather, rooks and grouse whirring, and the first sounds of the nearby farms awakening. When they turned and began climbing the hillside, sheep reared up and ran bleating into the gorse. The children leapt nimble on the rocks, following until they were in a sea of heather. The purple sunswept ground, dry and brittle underfoot, was patched with tangles of tall bracken and low-lying hollows of brilliant green marsh which had to be skirted on their way to the summit. Butterflies hovered in the ling and banked away from their scudding feet as they raced upwards. It was a long climb. May collapsed and fell panting in a clump of bilberries to slake her thirst on a handful of gleaming berries. The juice stained her fingers and her tongue bright maroon. Matt stood laughing nearby, throwing stones down the hill.

The morning grew warmer and shrouds of midst gradually cleared from distant tracts of woodland and fields. Nestled in dry grass the children rested, letting the welcome heat seep into their bodies. May, yawning, pushed her reddened fingers through her hair, ruffling the damp strands which clung to her forehead. She spread her coat out and lay carelessly, her hands behind her head, listening to the minute rustling of insects in the heath.

As the sun climbed higher in the clear blue sky the rocks grew warm to the touch. Matt took off his shoes and went off exploring nearby. He trod carefully, avoiding the spines of the gorse and the cutting edges of loose fragments of stone.

There were flecks of silica in the grit, reflecting the brilliant light like a myriad of mirrors, and deep ruts and indentations worn into the boulders by intense weathering, thousands of years of cracking ice and relentless summers' heat. He could see minute slivers of crystal trapped in these rivulets, over which the last few drops of the heavy dew were gathering to trickle down into the shade. At the base of the cracks he found strange and enchanted looking rock plants, sage green, lime and silver, cushioned in pads of moss.

These miniature kingdoms were host to glossy beetles, chafers and stag-horns, and over them hovered dun coloured moths and crane flies. They were all fragile, darting, elusive. The air seemed to be alive with the sound of quivering wings, millions of antennae searching out the nectar from the moor in its brief summer.

May drowsed until she felt thirsty and, calling Matt, set off in search of a stream. They drank the peat-tasting water and ate their packets of food, with their legs trailing in the icy brook.

"Ah think we've gone dumbstruck," May said shyly as she dried her feet with handfuls of grass. She threw the grass into the stream and watched it being carried away.

"We 'aven't said much, 'ave we? Nobody's said a word since we got here, 'ave they?"

Matt looked down. "It doesn't feel like you 'ave to talk or say owt up 'ere on t'moor. Well, I 'aven't had owt to say." He flushed, "Leastways, nuthin' ah felt like saying." ·

"Ah don't understand thee," she said quietly; "Yer can say anythin' yer like to me, ah's not stoppin' thee."

"It's not that, May, ah'd tell thee owt, thar knows that. It's just that great lumps o' stuff comes into yer brain, but it's not stuff yer can talk about. It rolls about in yer 'ead and then when you've thought about it, it sticks in your throat and won't come out. It's daft, anyway, you'd feel a gorm." His voice trailed away.

"Like what sort o' things?" she asked, turning her head and looking at him directly.

He looked steadfastly at the ground. "Ah can't say, not properly. It comes out of being on the moor, or when we're in our own wood, that's when it happens; Ah gets like this."

He burrowed his face down into the heather. The scent of the moor and the fierce mid-day sun imprisoned him in a day dream, burning an image into his brain.

A transparent replica of his body floated away. He ran after it, trying to catch it. It was like a balloon, moving slowly through a haze. He caught it, crumpled it and rolled it into a ball. Falling onto his knees, he pushed it into the ground, which mysteriously opened to receive it. It travelled on its own impetus through fibrous roots and damp peat and remained deep down, buried like treasure, and only he knew where it was.

May leapt across the stream and ran towards a birch tree some distance away. She climbed and stood straddle-legged in the dappled shade, shaking the silver leaves in a flurry of light. Matt stood up and slowly walked over to the trees. She stood still now in the branches and looked down at him calmly.

"You know what I mean, Matt Bedford. There's something between us, isn't there? It shouldn't be up to the girl to say, should it?"

There was a long pause. He began picking with a fingernail at the tree trunk, peeling the wafer-like bark away in a delicate ribbon.

"All this, look," he said, staring across the moor, "and all that out there, it wouldn't be the same without you, May."

After a while they began the walk back to Stanedge where their bicycles were hidden in the bracken. They held hands, but neither looked at each other, and Matt whistled to himself.

"Do you think we're together?" he shouted as they cycled down the lane, "Do you think I can be your lad?"

"Thar can, if thar wants me ter be thy lass," May called back, "Ah thinks thar a bit young fo' me though," she laughed, "Lads don't grow up as quick as lasses."

Chapter XX

DARK DAYS

Jess elected to go down the pit again when the general call-up began. Other men who did not wish to face conscription went with him back to the seam. After years of freedom from the colliery the rush downwards in the black cage to the foul galleries and passages below was like a daily prison sentence, but preferable to an exile in khaki far away. The colliery worked three shifts round the clock, racing to keep up the tonnage quota for the steelworks and foundries, the men on a punishing rota which barely gave them time to become accustomed to working nights before they found themselves back on days.

The blitz over Sheffield was the nearest that war came. At night the village turned out and congregated in the allotments by the far row to watch the lurid pall of red in the sky twenty miles to the north. It would begin as a thin stain on the horizon and gradually build until there was a furnace glow, rent with the blasts of explosions and shooting tracers. A low-flying crippled German plane looped over the fields once, released a stick of bombs into the quarry and careered towards the wood where it crashed and burst into flames, destroying several acres of oak and beech in a fire that tore through the tinder-dry trees and bracken. It was days before the Home Guard could get near the shattered remnants of the aeroplane and its hideous charred contents. They dug a pit in the scorched earth when the corpses had been removed and hid what they could of the remainder.

Young Jack Drew joined up and went to serve in the Far East and one of the Bates boys spent the war in the cold waters of the North Sea, miraculously rescued every time the aircraft carriers and frigates he sailed in were destroyed.

A team of Bevin Boys, spindly youths recruited from distant parts, arrived in the village. They were lodged with local families, as were straggly groups of London evacuees, who were pale-skinned and whining of voice, brutalized by being wrenched from their families and surroundings, and alarmed at the raucous curiosity of their new schoolmates. The locals thought they were being kind if they managed to fix a billet on a farm, thought the fresh air would be good for them and the wholesome food build them up. But these city children were terrified of a herd of bullocks, ran a mile from a few sheep, and lay in bed at nights with the covers pulled up tight over their heads to muffle the owls and nightjars.

When rationing of food started, the villagers took it as a joke. There was still the occasional pig for slaughter, with pies, brawn, black puddings to share as well as the hams and sides of bacon; the Yates boys could always supply a rabbit, there were blackberries and mushrooms for the picking. But when the shortages began to hit, it was hard to make a few ounces of lard and sugar go round a big family, and the hot mugs of tea stiff with sugar which the miners needed to quench their thirst and wash down the dust were guarded jealously while the rest went to the tap.

Ma Bedford opened early on the first Sunday of the month when the new sweet coupons would be handed over. The children queued down her path most of the morning, clutching the precious little vouchers and whatever pennies they had managed to lever from their money boxes with a kitchen knife, looking forward to an orgy of acid drops and caramels. The pleasure had to be overwhelming enough to last in the memory for four whole weeks until the next assault on their taste buds could hold them in thrall.

Jess carried on with the forays into the country when work at the mine allowed, bringing back what foodstuffs could be spared on the horse-cart, and perhaps a miner who kept chickens in his backyard would part with a few eggs.

The children worked on the farms in the school holidays. At threshing time they were paid a penny a tail for the rats they managed to kill with a stick, or for a nest of young ones, pink and hairless, which would be thrown to the dogs.

They picked fields of potatoes, cut the tops off swedes and mangles, lifted sugar beet and burned the corn stubble. Sometimes there would be a clutch of plover's eggs camouflaged in the grass when they helped with the mowing, a hare streaking across a field towards a stream of pellets. They watched shire horses and cattle mating in season, and the birth of calves and piglets, watched when a broody hen or an old cockerel was despatched with a sharp wring of the neck.

The hard pressed farmers were grateful for the extra hands and sent the children home with a few shillings and cans of fresh milk, or took them back on wagons if it was dark before they finished.

One evening as they trailed back to the village at dusk they heard the sound of a warning klaxon from the pit-head and saw the thin column of steam rising from the apparatus high on the wheel housing. When they reached the sidings they climbed the rail and took the short cut through the yards towards the pit-head. Women and old men were already gathered there, and the off-duty deputies, in their ordinary clothes, had opened up the lamp shop for helmets and equipment and were making ready for a descent.

There had been a bad fall in the seam, an old working that had been re-opened, trapping a dozen men two miles from the shaft base.

Jess Bedford was one of them, Matt heard. Suddenly Ma Bedford was there with her broad arm round the boy, speechless and quivering. The wives of the other trapped men collected together, mute and deathsomely afraid.

They waited all night but there was no news from below. The cage was lowered and raised several times to take down heavy gear and relief workers. Occasionally a deputy approached the crowd, but there was little information he could pass on.

Ma Bedford was frustrated with the waiting. It made her feel useless, there were better things to be getting on with. She took firm hold of Matt and led him away up the gantry. Through the night she brewed up tea, to hell with the rations she thought, and made sandwiches which Matt ferried to the pit-head.

The men were trapped for three days in all. The women rumbled among themselves, remembering bits of information they had heard from the men, barely noticed at the time; the shortage of timber and its poor quality, eking out the props which were needed for shoring up roofs and shuttering the walls of new passages.

Ambulances had waited throughout the emergency. As the men were brought up from the ground after a way had been cut for them to scramble out on their bellies, the white-coated attendants ran forward with stretchers, but the weary miners waved them aside. A few were injured, a broken arm, crushed fingers, a gashed leg, but nothing so serious that they would accept assistance in front of their womenfolk. It had been the terror of poisonous gas building up in the chamber that had worn them out. They raised a cheer for the crowd and gulped the fresh air, turning their squinting eyes to the sun, and realised that in a few days they would be going down again.

Chapter XXI

IF THE CAP FITS

Ma Bedford and Jess were elated when they heard that their son had won a scholarship to the Grammar School in the nearby town. She jigged up and down in the shop, hugged her neighbours, and prepared an extra special high tea with sherry trifle and Bakewell tarts, while he went over to wait for Matt at the village school gate.

"Thar's dun it lad, thar's bloody dun it, thar wain't be comin' 'ere no more. Thar goin' ter be a scholar," he grinned as he seized the boy before marching him towards the headmaster's room.

Mr. Evans was cautiously pleased. It was some vindication of his regime to have a boy accepted for his academic promise. The records showed that barely half a dozen pupils had won scholarships to the town since the school had opened, and there were certainly no parents in the village who could have afforded the considerable fees. He brushed the cigarette ash from his tie, coughed a little and rocked on his feet before answering. "It will be hard work, boy, and totally new to you. You will be at a severe disadvantage studying with boys who may have been at preparatory school. You may find that some of them can already decline and conjugate," he said, wagging a crooked finger at Matt.

He crossed to the window and watched the big wheel turning for the last cage ascent of the day.

"But remember your roots, boy, as I remember mine back in the Rhondda."

His Celtic blue eyes burnt into the boy as he shook hands. He wondered if this slip of a boy were destined to escape, slake his thirst of his surroundings and have done with them. Or would that gentle stranglehold never loosen its grip, as it never had loosed on himself.

"Come and see me whenever you like," he said kindly, opening the door.

As Jess and Matt walked across the empty playground Mr. Evans lit another cigarette and reflected gratefully that the torrent of memories of his own youth which had stormed through his frame, interrupting the interview so uncomfortably, had at least prevented him from making too many unwitting platitudes. And at the moment he stared at the boy so fiercely, feeling so hopelessly uncommunicative, but longing to dredge up some valuable words of advice and encouragement, nevertheless there had been a fusion of images in his brain, a certain kind of metamorphosis of unspoken elements which might eventually redeem his unforgivable lack of articulacy. Remembered sights, sounds and sensations came swimming in his brain, melting together into some new material under the catalystic action of the muse which was his birthright from a long line of Druids and Non-conformists. Burning corn on a steep hillside, the smell of wet overcoats in a vestibule, loud harmonious singing under corrugated roofs. He took up a pen, pleased with himself. It was going to be a good prose poem, full of hwyl, if he could just catch it and get it on the page.

There were no such literary considerations for Ma Bedford. Her main preoccupation over the next few days was with the required list of uniform and equipment from the official stockist in the High Street. To Matt it was a confusing plethora of black barathea and grey flannel garments, striped socks and ties, name tags, cricket bats and hockey sticks, parcels and boxes of stuff which all had to be tried on and fitted in the sticky confines of the changing room of the Junior Department of Messrs. Swallows, Outfitters to the Gentry and the Public.

On the first day of term he was dressed up early and sent over to Ma Drew to show her the full effect and gained half a crown. It was an uncomfortable moment, having politely refused, seeing the arthritic hand, twisted from so much kneeding and mangling, push the coin into his top pocket, and noting the curious pale watering of the old lady's eyes. There were a few jokes from Old Man Drew and then it was away to the bus, feeling sick with nerves and apprehension.

The town was awash with hordes of boys jostling with their satchels towards the Sheffield Road, and more sedate groups of girls twittering under their shining new straw boaters making for the adjoining High School. The new boys were conspicuous in their fresh smart rig-outs, the smaller ones quite obviously fitted in several sizes too large to allow for growth. A surprising number wore spectacles with thick lenses and some had wire braces on their teeth with the effect that they looked more like oversized beetles than undersized boys, scurrying along in their black peaked caps. The school prefects lounged gracefully at street corners along the principal route through the town, quiffed and laconic, occasionally stirring themselves to aim a deft kick at some over-boisterous or dawdling youth. As far as the eye could see the black and grey crocodile streamed down the road past the high stone wall, and Matt was swept along by the tide until it wheeled through the gates and on to the emerald quadrangle.

The noise and fooling died away before the serried ranks of the masters who stood in silence on the steps eyeing the newcomers. For a few awesome moments the only movement was the billowing of their gowns and the rustling of sheaves of paper in the breeze, until the rosters were called, orders barked out, and the boys ran into their lines with a clockwork precision that would have graced a military operation.

It was quite clear to Matt which one of the masters would announce himself to be Head. He was the very tall one, a vast bulk of silk with enormous clasped hands, purple face and downdrawn mouth. His very weight and physical presence proclaimed his authority as did the decisive short cough he made before his address.

The boys were soon ushered away to their formrooms, divided into cells, as Matt's headmaster put it, to begin the process of indoctrination.

The next few weeks were bewildering for the new boys, especially the scholarship boys like Matt who came from rural districts and were unfamiliar with form divisions, rotas, complex timetables and the unwritten rules and customs of such an ancient establishment, but they soon settled into the strange surroundings and learned quickly how to dodge the worst punishments of the system. Since ignorance could never be offered as an excuse, the secrets of the freemasonry had somehow to be prised from sympathetic older boys, or learned from scufflings from prefects.

There were fights, forbidden on threat of expulsion, secretly convened in the lavatories or in the concrete fives court while the pecking order of the newcomers was asserted in dangerous games of initiation, broken teeth and bloodied noses.

To Matt it all seemed very remote from the peaceful class in the village. There were no flowers on windowsills, charts or wallhangings, and the old corridors and lecture rooms reeked of neglect. But there was a challenge in the new work and the stimulus of fresh companions. He gradually became absorbed into the system and started to lead a strange double life. After school he changed out of his uniform and was a village boy. And once a week there was a glorious release when Matt and a small group of friends cut dinner to hear Lockhart's organ practice in the Parish Church. They were choristers, working acolytes who knew and loved every stone and echo of the fabric, mindful of the tranquility of the venerable transepts and still in awe of the church's majesty.

Lockhart would climb the winding staircase to the loft holding his battered briefcase full of manuscripts, dubbed the Holy Relics by the other boys, while the rest wandered silently about or sat in a dark corner waiting.

There is a particular silence about such places. Between soaring arches and in the curved lofty spaces of vaulted roofs, the murmurings of past and present prayers, litanies, careful footsteps, bells and intonations have mingled with the dust and the incense into a perpetual state of reverberation. Faint sounds penetrating from outside leave their own imprint on the existing polyphony and bird song in the gardens filters through the stained glass to add to the testament. Not a real silence, but an endless and flowing pattern of small sounds and cadences which invades the head and focuses the spirit.

So it was with a sense of wonder the boys entered the church, each falling into his own sense of rapture at the mysterious and beautiful aura of the interior. Matt would run his fingers along the smooth alabaster limbs and feet of the polished statuary of the tombs and linger over the beeswaxed tracery of screens and grillwork. The Lady Chapel, blue and gold, cool in its verdant simplicity, was a special haven in which to sit listening to Lockhart's practice. There was a high gilded reredos and an altar hanging worked in soft coloured wools depicting beasts of the field, lilies and acanthus leaves, and the Host was displayed in a niche illuminated by a candle in a crimson glass saucer.

After the distant sounds of the bellows and stops and the cranking up of the stool, the music would come cascading over the choir stalls and fill the dim corner, washing the grey stone and the embroideries with strange magnificence. The Virgin gazed down from her pedestal with limpid eyes frozen in an expression of infinite compassion. She wore a white wimple edged with gold thread and a dress of cornflower blue which brushed her chipped plaster feet.

As the huge chords mounted, swaying upwards in deafening spirals of echoes, Matt surrendered to the power of the music and his imagination. He became the figurehead of a galleon ploughing through mountainous waves, a great bird cresting on powerful wings over an endless forest, a wind surging over high mountains. He was a cathedral builder, conjuring pinnacles, turrets and spires over an empty plain and then a painter emblazoning the interior with ravishing designs.

When the music died away much of the glory rolled away in the diminuendo. The dense silence returned, broken by the noise of the shutters in the organ loft and Lockhart clumping down the narrow winding staircase. The boys would gather in the porch and drift back to school, idly chatting. They were perhaps a little more quiet than usual, part of their minds still engrossed by the splendours, and their arms were around each other's shoulders.

Chapter XXII

BALL GAMES

"Get down from theer, you dirty buggers. What yer peepin' at, eh? I know what you're up to. Come on, get down and be off 'ome."

It was Mona clacking across the pub yard in her peep-toe wedge-heeled sling backs, her costume a vivid clash of magenta and spruce green. The mock crocodile raincoat she wore, slung around her shoulders, flapped like the wings of a vampire bat. A crowd of kids were standing tip-toe on the benches outside the clubroom of the pub, having a good look at the football teams stripping off for the Saturday game.

She flayed at them with her new plastic handbag, saving a special clout for her son Norman and a good tug at Brenda's ginger hair. "Disgusting! Naked men in there, yer shouldn't be gawpin' an' peepin' like that; where's yer manners? Anybody 'ould think you'd bin dragged up. You two just wait till yer feyther gets to 'ear about this."

The boys ran off whooping to a safe distance, jostled into the bus shelter and lit a few fags. Mona stood glaring at them. Her huge teeth and carmine lips formed a gash in her chalky powdered face, like a silent scream. She was in a hurry on her way into town, anxious to get there before the pubs closed, and now she had the extra aggravation of this indecent carry-on.

Having rushed through the morning chores, the piles of pit clothes, rinsing, mangling and hanging out to dry, as well as throwing some food together for the hungry hordes, she had precious little time for her toilette. Her hair was still in curlers, but squashed into a useful jersey turban, and in the haste to get out, her eyebrow pencil had slipped rather badly. Not her usual polished and manicured appearance, but not bad for a rushed job, and she had a few quid in her bag to spend thank God. But now this extra piggish irritation and those hideous grinning lads.

"She's a right one ter talk," Reuben prodded Norman. "Ah thought thi' muther liked a bit o'dick. If we wern't 'ere she'd 'ave 'ad a bloody good look 'ersen."

When the bus came Mona stalked forward with some dignity, smiling at the conductor. She was glad to be getting out of this hell-hole, and was looking forward to a nice afternoon in the Station Hotel with a better class of person. Perhaps that nice salesman from Leicester would be in the snug. She unwrapped a mint lump and chomped contentedly in anticipation.

As soon as the bus rounded the corner and disappeared from view the kids returned to their vantage point. The room had a tattered, though vaguely festive appearance. The ceiling was decorated with a few dusty paper chains and half-shrivelled balloons and at one end of the room there was a small platform on which stood a battered upright piano and a drum kit. The local team and the visitors had staked out opposite sides of the hall. They were full of beer from a good session in the bar next door, and looking forward to a good game. There was no false modesty from these men who were accustomed to working half-naked in the pits and standing in the tub in front of the fire to get washed when they came home. They stripped off and folded their Saturday clothes in neat piles and strolled about, joking, full of bravado against the opposing team. The children pressed their noses to the windows relishing the free peep-show. It was quite a comic spectacle, a collection of those funny blokes on picture postcards from the seaside. Knobbly knees, paunchy bellies and scrawny necks, hammer toes, pimply bums, hairy chests, and best of all, those bushy bits and screamingly funny wobbling, dangling, long, thin, fat, screwed-up buttony, blobby things. The children held their sides as they ached from tittering, falling in helpless fits of giggling. A little girl wet her knickers and had to run home, and the boys laughed till they cried when they saw the stream of piddle she had left on the bench. It was better than the pictures, they thought, and they gave a rousing, if hoarse, cheer, choking on their laughter, when the teams trotted out and made off for the pitch.

It was the usual rough game. A few fights and thumps of course, plenty of swearing and jostling, and one nasty incident when a fat lad from Duckmanton got kicked in the balls and lost one up inside. The referee blew his whistle and stopped the game for a few minutes. Everyone, including the tea ladies streamed on to the field, cursing the cow-shit and splattering their stockings with muck. They gathered round shouting encouragement as the ref yanked the shorts off the groaning perspiring youth, looking for the missing nut. He pressed and prodded the groin while one of the ladies applied a wet teacloth to the affected part, and eventually, with the lad screaming like a stuck pig, the lost object popped back into its rightful place.

At half-time the ladies provided quarters of lemon to suck and slapped their own lads on the back, glowering the while at the rough lot from Duckmanton. Ma Lawton glared at the hefty full-back who had floored Sid and whacked that poor little Dennis Fletcher.

"They can't 'elp it love," she confided loudly to Mrs. Bates, "they live like animals up there. Wouldn't care for it meself. They're that mucky even t'bugs daren't come out t'wallpaper." "Oh, ah've 'eard," replied Mrs. Bates, loud enough for the heaving player to hear. "Our Doris were disgusted wi' it, she only stopped theer a week afore she were back wi' me. Mam, she said, yer wouldn't believe what ah've seen in Duckmanton. Oh ay, she were glad ter get back 'ere. 'Er Fred were chuffed an' all. T'pigs runnin' in t'ouses and t'fowls, and they never empty t'middens. It fair stinks, she said. Made 'er feel badly."

The full-back had heard more than enough. Full to the craw, he lunged towards the pair of them, but the whistle blew for the second half and all he could manage was a string of oaths. As he veered down the field, relieved it hadn't come to blows, the ladies yelled out to the home team. "Come on lads, kick 'em, crucify 'em, we'll show 'em who's boss."

The match reeled to an inglorious end and the players took their bruises off to the clubroom and the waiting bottles of liniment. The trouble with a draw was that the whole bloody thing had got to be gone through again.

In the evening everyone repaired to the same room for a dance. Phyllis Laycock took saxophone and Herbert Hargreaves obliged on the drums. A variety of pianists took turns about, according to which musical numbers they were familiar with. Rita Sharp, wearing a very effective crepe dress cut low in front and some new marcasites revealed an unexpected talent for ballads. Her father, who was a strong member of the Parish Council, accepted various compliments quite gracefully on her behalf, but inside he was raging, desperate to find out where she had learned all that trash. When he nailed her by the tea urn in the refreshment room, at first she made out that she had heard the numbers on the radio when she sat knitting with Grace, her sister-in-law, but when pressed, finally admitted to having spent some Saturday evenings in the Co-op hall in town learning the new jive. But these new fangled dances had not arrived yet in the village. The evening was taken up with Moonlight Saunters, the Violet Tango, Hesitation Waltz, Military Two-Step and other old favourites.

Ma Bedford was in charge of the catering. She presided behind a series of trestle tables ladened with vanilla slices, sausage rolls and lemon curd tarts, all at twopence apiece, proceeds towards the new seat in the cemetery. There was a spot dance and a lucky draw, excuse-mes, and a Paul Jones.

Matt led Monica through the Barn Dance on Rose's insistence, otherwise he was content to go round the floor with May, who was fairly expert, having learned from her big cousin Enid who lived at Tibshelf where they had a weekly affair in the Working Men's Club.

Herbert seemed to be in a trance on the drums. The boys got together in a corner, laying bets as to whether he would drop off, but he managed to keep the same insistent beat going, and produced the odd surprising juggling trick with the drum sticks.

The boys seemed to have a better time than the girls who had to keep nipping off to the convenience, errands of mystery which involved pins and borrowed elastic. At least the lads had their shandies and the brave talk about what they were going to do on the walk home with the girls. It was only spoilt when the M.C., announced a ladies' invitation St. Bernards

Waltz. The older women got to their feet and advanced towards the young bloods with inviting smiles. They reeked of cologne and lily of the valley, towering over their junior partners with formidable elegance. The worst part was the squashy roll of fat which stuck out over the top of the corset, which was just the place a determined lady would firmly place a boy's right hand.

The evening was enjoyed by all, the *Derbyshire Times* reported next week, and the fund for the new cemetery seat had been increased by a grand total of two pounds seven and sixpence, winner of the tea cosy Miss Deborah Kershaw, spot waltz Mr. & Mrs. Frank Barlow.

ESSAY — MATT BEDFORD

Write at least one page about a local historic monument. — Ancient Remains at Temple Normanton.

The present church in our village is a wooden structure which dates only from the late nineteenth century. It was built to replace an earlier church which was destroyed by fire. The decision to put up a wooden building was made on account of the area being subject to subsidence as a result of mining for coal underneath. Some of the stones from the early church are stored in a barn nearby. The barn itself is an interesting example of an early tithe barn. It is one side of the courtyard of a ruined manor house which is supposed to be the remains of a lodge once occupied by the Knights Templar. The Royal Oak in Chesterfield was the headquarters of this group of Knights and they travelled from there on their crusades. The stones are piled in the corner of the upstairs half of the barn. Many are carved. There are also fragments of stained glass with the original lead. Across the road from the manor house there is a small field surrounded by a drystone wall. Local boys were digging once and uncovered part of a tiled floor which was thought to be Roman. There are many humps and mounds in the field, which looks as though it could have been quarried or opencasted, but the site could be excavated for further evidence. Nearby are the ruins and gardens of the old part of the village which has been abandoned. They are crofts which were lived in by farm workers until 1900.

Chapter XXIII

LETTER FROM AMERICA

Mona came properly into her own with the Army build-up. Great covered lorries began churning through the countryside, spilling thousands of raw boned recruits to bivouac into the Home Parks of nearby stately houses. The girls waited on the top road to wave to the lads bound for Hardwick Hall. During the following weeks they got bolder, twirling in their folkweave dirndls and throwing up their legs like can-can dancers. As the camouflaged vans sped by they yelled out to the pimply lads who hung cheering out of the back; Geordies, Brummagers and Scousers who shouted back in thick foreign dialects, incomprehensible without the clear accompanying gestures.

They began turning up in the dance halls in town, always in numbers for safety and nervous of upsetting the burly local lads. The girls sat in decorous rows, eyeing the newcomers. Nice boys, they thought, well turned out in their webbing and khaki, polished boots and Brylcreemed partings, alright for a bit of a cuddle in a shop doorway before the last bus home.

Mona was thrilled with the rush of new blood. She walked the arcades with a new confidence; pick and choose was her motto, and these lads should be grateful she was a lady. Her heels got higher, and the kick-pleat more daring. She acquired a silver fox and wore it draped over a shoulder like Joan Crawford and perched a smart little felt hat, trimmed with a wisp of veiling, forward and to one side over her new upswept hair style. Sometimes she held court in the Wine Vaults in the Shambles allowing a nice young man to buy her a port and lemon to sip as she cast her eye around, wondering who was her best bet. Not for her an amateurish affair in a dark alley, but the comfort of the back upstairs room at the George and then a few drinks with the landlord after closing time.

The village girls were less ambitious and sometimes rounded off an evening by being pedalled home on the cross-bar of a stolen bicycle. There would be a quick last breathless kiss at the top of the hill and the young soldier would speed off towards Hardwick, hoping to make it before the gates closed. With any luck there would be no questions from the M.P.s and he could throw the bike into the ornamental lake where it would rust away under the lily pads with a hundred others until the end of the war.

The Americans, when they finally arrived, were a very different proposition. Smooth of complexion, almost jaundiced in their fading tans, they were sleek and fat, well fed and bulging in their neat gabardines. They had thick creaseless necks, enormous capable hands and mouthfuls of gleaming white teeth. They drawled politely, prettily narrowing their pale blue, far-seeing Western eyes, devastating the locals with their 'sirs' and 'ma'ams', and were generous to a fault.

The children were happy enough at first to scrabble for the tins of powdered coffee and chocolate bars which the newcomers threw from the windows of the troop trains, but when the novelty wore off there were better games to play, and anyway the coffee was bitter.

When village romance began in earnest between the local lasses and their new idols, it was good to pretend to be fobbed off by a couple of oranges or a packet of chewing gum and let an unsuspecting sister or cousin lead her beau away to a secret courting spot. Then treacherously follow, sneaking up the long way round hedgerows and dykes, to be a hidden guest at the feast when the girl parted her thighs in the clover field.

After the soldier had squeezed himself back into his floral shorts and hauled the dazed girl to her feet to moon back to the village, there was sometimes a curious knotted pink rubber object and a torn foil wrapper half-hidden in the trampled grass or stuffed into a scrumpled Chesterfield packet.

"Ay up, look 'ere."

"What's thar got?"

"French letter."

"What is it?"

"T' Yank 'ad it on when 'e were shaggin' 'er."

"What for?"

"Stop 'er from 'aving a babby."

"Ow?"

"Stop's spunk, look sithee."

"Look 'ere, gormless, this stuff in t'teat at t'end."

"Looks like goss."

"Dare thee ter oppen it up. Untie t'knot."

"Bollocks, thar waint get me touchin' that, it's germy."

"Pick it up wi' a stick then."

Later, doshing in a pool in the dammed up brook, shivering in the cold muddy water.

"Wash it aht, an' we'll blow it up like a balloon."

"Thar can, if thar wants, ah'm not shovin' that in my gob."

"Fancy your Rosemary 'avin' that up 'er crack. Ah bet she'd drop dead if she knew we'd seen 'em at it."

"She's goin' ter 'ave ter treat me or else ah shall tell 'er ah'm goin' ter tell mi mam."

"Ay, an' not just thee, we brought thee, din't wi?"

Quite some young ladies had to delve deep into their purses after surrendering to the occupying force and a good number of lads got to see the latest Tyrone Power or Betty Grable. It was all in a good cause.

Chapter XXIV
CEREMONIALS

The Barlows were out when the boy arrived on a bike from Chesterfield with the wire about Reg. They had gone off for the day to Matlock; a rare outing all together, in their best clothes, looking for a picnic on High Tor and a visit to the Petrifying Well.

The nearest neighbour signed for the telegram and went up the road trembling to wait by the bus stop.

The message was straightforward and cruelly brief, posted from Catterick, timed and dated early that morning. It seemed that Reg had been involved in a tragic and completely unforseeable accident on a training exercise, that every precaution had been taken, and the body would be delivered for burial when the proper arrangements had been made, etc.

Mrs. Barlow went upstairs to draw the curtains while Frank went to the coalhouse with the bucket. May made the tea and the brothers sat around the kitchen table in their stiff collars, empty-eyed.

The news filtered through the village and into the Jacksons who wondered whether to write to Clarice, but decided to wait for a while. Ma Bedford occupied herself with the catering for Saturday's wedding, Freda Wormsley to Harriet Greaves' youngest from Bolsover.

On the day, the funeral took place early, and the villagers, apart from close family mourners, had a few hours to change into more festive clothing and put themselves in a different mood for the later affair, since everyone wanted to give Freda a good send off.

Matt left the tea party and wandered down the street to the Barlows. Frank saw him through the slit in the drawn curtain.

"Thy lad's come lookin' fo' thee," he said expressionlessly, "thar ought ter get thissen of wi' 'im fer a bit of a blow."

May left her parents to the fire and the ticking clock and her brothers aimlessly pottering in the coop with their pigeons. The two went over to the recreation ground and drifted round on the Red Emma, listening to the singing coming from the Working Men's Club.

It was odd to hear the familiar choruses coming across the field, laughter rising in distant crescendos and the faint sound of the gavel banging for the speeches.

Ripples of applause hung in the air intermittently, breaking the silence between the pair while Matt tried to frame his words.

The sounds were unfocussed and remote but they made a strangely comforting accompaniment to the motion of the roundabout.

Soon the wedding party spilled out into the gardens to pose for photographs and afterwards, Freda walked up the hill to the cemetery where she laid her bridal bouquet of white roses on Reg's grave.

Chapter XXV
WHAT CAN I GET YOU?

They were men of the world at fourteen, they thought, especially on Saturday mornings when the young social aspirants of the town and district met for the parade under the arches on High Pavement.

The costume, de rigueur, was tweed hacking jacket and flannels, linen shirt and silk cravat, the posture casual. A good effect could be achieved by lounging outside the Victoria Cinema in a pose similar to the one taken by the leading actor on the poster for the latest attraction.

The Art School mob contrived a more flamboyant style with capes and carefully paint-splashed smocks, while the Labour League of Youth, handing out their hand printed leaflets, cut a dash with their long hair, red ties and consciously open vowels.

When it came to the girls, Matt discovered that it was a tactical error to speak too soon. They had to be avoided until after the throng had drifted into the Victoria Tea Room for cups of weak coffee and lifeless buns. Then it was alright to stroll over, chatting with a friend about the new play at the Civic or last night's Hallé concert in Sheffield, give the merest glance and move on, hoping the girl in question would blush, lower her head, turn round, or give out any other minute signal of lust. She had to be made to wait then until the parade took to the arches once more, when a boy might just accidentally step backwards and bump into her or drop a book at her feet.

Such a chance encounter often led to an exciting afternoon at Gladys Anscombe's Latin American class for juniors, or tennis and lemonade in the municipal park, depending on the weather.

But these High School and Convent girls were a little pale and earnest for Matt's taste. He could never get them, for example, to venture into the Co-op Hall on Saturday nights for the jive.

It was here he met Ellie while Ma Bedford thought he was seeing Maria Montez in 'Gypsy Wildcat' at the Regal. She was dark haired and flushed from dancing, smelled of Knights Castile and perspiration, and carried a handkerchief which she used to dab cologne on the pit of her throat.

Ellie was very different from the other girls he had danced with in village schoolrooms. She pulled herself close to him and led his hands around the back of her mauve crepe dress and down over her buttocks, pressing her pelvis forward in motion with the music. Sometimes she closed her eyes and crooned along with the band, half smiling, her warm breath redolent of the little pink cachous she was sucking. Then, as if suddenly distracted or bored, she would hang on Matt's right shoulder and oblige him to go round the floor with her dancing the fashionable cruise step, shuffling forward side by side while she brazenly eyed the boys lined up on the walls.

Matt was in a turmoil over Ellie long before the end of the dance, thrilled by the heat of her body and her tight grasp, but churned up by these sudden moods of inattention, and he hated the loafing youths who nudged each other and winked at Ellie every time they came round. For quite a while she disappeared and he squashed himself into a corner near the band trying to look as though he was cooling off and enjoying the antics of the players. He caught sight of her in the side room where a bar had been set up on trestles. She was drinking a light ale, giggling with a couple of girls. When she turned and saw him crouched at the table she waved, spilling some of the beer, and after whispering to her friends, brought them over to be introduced.

"Sorry luv, I don't know yer name yet do I, but then, it's early days yet, isn't it? This is Wilma and Enid."

Matt mumbled his name, drowned by the band striking up the next number, and Enid dragged him on to the floor drawling "Come and glide with me, snake."

Towards the end of the evening the crowd broke up with a scattering of applause. The bandleader allowed a decent pause, just long enough to allow the clientele to sort themselves out for the last waltz. Youths who had not danced all night made a last brave attempt to partner up with the girls they had been lusting for all evening

The wallflowers got up sadly in pairs, clutching their handbags and outdoor shoes in anticipation of the rush at the door and the charge through town for the last buses.

Matt flushed and waited anxiously for Ellie who had excused herself and trotted off to the cloakroom. To his surprise she came out in her overcoat and headscarf ready to leave. She jerked her head indicating he should follow and went through the swing doors with a wave to Enid and Wilma.

He ran after her and followed her clattering footsteps down the stairs to the pavement. She grabbed his hand tightly.

"Come on love, we've got a bus to catch, let's not muck about. We'll 'ave a few minutes if we get off now."

They sped through the alleys of the Shambles and made a short cut diagonally across the church yard, running hand in hand till they arrived in a back street behind the bus station. Ellie pulled Matt into a darkened doorway away from the street lamps. They were both panting furiously from the run, but she rose on her tip toes and squeezed her mouth over his. Her hands roamed over his body and the hardness in his flannels where she lingered and squeezed. He shook violently at the immediate flow from his body and again she took his hand and pulled it down to her hem and then upwards. His eyes were closed, his head buried in her neck as he fumbled with her underwear and found his way through. He was shocked to find hair where it should have been smooth like marble, and for a moment froze, trembling. But she pressed on his hand and wriggled her hips around urgently until his fingers went lower down and he felt the moist between her thighs. She arched her thin back, whimpering in his ear, and the smells of powder, lipstick, cachous and cologne compressed themselves into the quivering sound.

Pounding footsteps raced by the doorway. They both straightened their clothes and ran following into the brightly lit compound of the station. For a second they held hands tightly before they dashed for their separate buses and waved to each other from the top deck.

On the following Wednesday, Ma Bedford's half-day, Matt was to meet his mother in town after school as usual. "Ah'll be on t'Market Hall steps, duck, about four; ah'll 'ave 'ad mi 'air done at Elsie's by then. Wi can 'ave a good look round and then 'ave us tea. Ah like a good fuddle. Tarrah."

She loved the brief outings with her son in the busy market town. There was the opportunity of running into a few of her old mates from the mill where she had worked as a girl, or customers who had left the village for other districts. Then there was a chance, picking a way through what was left of the market, of coming across a few bargains before they went on to the cinema or a tea shop.

"Ah fancy a fish tea meself," she announced with some finality when she had completed her purchases. There was a pound of tripe, a pork pie, a pair of corsets and a bundle of cauliflower plants for Jess.

"Come on," she said, bundling it all into a carrier bag, "We'll get a nice place in t'window at Woodheads if we nip."

The tea room was already crowded with ample ladies tucking into vast platefuls of halibut. The little cane tables seemed too insubstantial for the massed gilt and white china, silver tea pots and cut glass stands piled with cream horns.

Ma Bedford and Matt squeezed through the tables towards the window, stepping over the laden shopping bags and baskets which spilled over the Turkey carpet, and settled down to pore over the menu. Decisions made, it was pleasant to relax in anticipation of delicious food and a pot of special blend, and watch the world go by down Packers Row outside.

There suddenly was a small voice by their side. "What can ah get yer, Mrs. Bedford, 'ave yer made yer mind up yet?" Something like a blast in a furnace exploded in Matt's chest, sending shock waves outwards to his ear drums. Colour flew to his face, and his ears were stained like a cockscomb. The menu had fluttered to the floor. He bent down, taking much more time than he needed to retrieve it, in order to regain something approaching composure. His eyes fixed on a pair of slim legs clad in black silk stockings under a pencil skirt over which dangled a ridiculously small rounded apron edged with broderie anglaise. When he was brave enough to stop fishing about under the table, and straightened up to replace the menu, wedging it between the crockery, even though he offered up a silent prayer for a miracle to wipe the day off the slate, the ceiling to crash in or his rabbits to die, there was Ellie, seemingly calm though a little flushed, and studiously avoiding him. She took the order, turned and flounced towards the swing doors into the back room.

"Do ah know that young woman?" Ma Bedford asked. "Ah don't remember seein' 'er in 'ere before, do you luv? Anyway she's very pleasant, got a nice way with 'er."

With that she took a slice of bread and butter and chewed thoughtfully. "Per'aps she knows you, duck. 'Ave you come across 'er, that she know'd my name." The question did not really seem to require an answer, Matt was relieved to feel. His mother appeared to be ruminative enough, contentedly waiting for the fish.

He toyed with the cutlery and shuffled his feet, stealing the odd glance towards the serving hatch and the occasional glimpse of Ellie criss-crossing the clouds of steam from the urn.

She served the meal up very professionally, cleared away nicely and brought the bill.

"That was lovely, duck," Ma Bedford exclaimed. "Our kid's enjoyed 'imself, 'aven't yer luv. Gotter feed 'im up. 'E's a growin' lad, yer know." She heaved herself to her feet, delving into her handbag. "And 'ere's sixpence for you, duck. Thank you, tarrah."

Ellie held open the door to let her out into the street, but managed to block the opening enough so that Matt had to squeeze past her to follow. She pressed her body forward imperceptibly, her hand brushing his thigh. In the lowest murmur she breathed "Ah wouldn't 'ave got that if she knew what we were up to Saturday." Then, more smiling, "Wor it worth it."

The next afternoon Matt changed his usual route across the town after school and tried to slip unnoticed down Packers Row. He loitered casually, pretending to scan a copy of the *Sheffield Star*, in a doorway opposite Woodheads.

There was no glimpse of Ellie. Perhaps, he thought, she had been put in the upstairs room, and he craned his neck towards the overhanging gable, but he could only make out a solitary diner in the window.

He crossed over the narrow street and walked past the cafe as slowly as he dared, still holding the newspaper open, and bumped into a young woman pushing a pram.

"Look out lad," she laughed, "It's worse than t'dodgems 'ere. Lookin' for a winner are thar?"

He mumbled an excuse and escaped into a nearby bookshop. The old door resented the speed of his entrance, setting up a loud clanging of bells followed by a heavy thud as it closed. The frowning owner, Mr. Frisby, looked up.

"What can I get you, young man?"

Matt looked anxiously about the shop. "Can I look round please?"

He dumped his satchel and the *Star* by the counter and retreated into the dark confines of the rear room where second-hand books were stacked in musty piles almost to the ceiling. "Some good stuff in there," came the voice more kindly. "Arnold Bennett, Brontes, Mrs. Gaskell, Ouida, ever heard of Ouida? It's all a bob in there, perhaps more like two and a tanner if you come across anything with good plates in it. Have a good look, no hurry, lad."

Matt pondered his predicament as he wandered along the racks, his hands in his pockets searching for coins, especially ones with milled edges. Mentally he added up his resources. He decided he could afford a modest purchase and while away a little time, bringing him nearer to the hour when Ellie might conceivably be leaving the cafe next door but one.

Mr. Frisby joined him in the recess, flicking a feather duster, ostensibly busying himself but rather glad of the company.

"Found anything you fancy, young man? Now here's something rather good for a local lad. *Sea and Sardinia*, D. H. Lawrence, born at Eastwood you know, one of us." He laughed, "Ever read any of the novels? *Plumed Serpent, White Peacock?*

He pulled a volume from a shelf and held it forward.

"Perhaps you're a bit young" he said thoughtfully, "but you'll come to it."

Matt spent a pleasant half-hour in the shop with Mr. Frisby, thanked him for his trouble and came out with a small morocco-bound account of the Eyam Plague and a monograph on Sickert, promising to come back next week when he was in better funds for the Aeneid translation, the George Burrowes and Izaak Walton.

Outside the chill evening had set in with sharp gusts of wind sending little flurries of rain into the pools of light cast by the gas brackets.

Matt huddled again in the sweetshop doorway, stuffing the new books into his satchel and stamping his feet against the cold.

The customers had all left the cafe opposite and a couple of the tables were now occupied by the waitresses dressed in their outdoor clothes, ready for clocking off. Ellie was placed with her back to the window, rocking in her chair, obviously enjoying some joke or other, and an elderly lady was larking about dancing. The steamed up window reduced her efforts to a dumb pantomime, but Matt could see clearly her grimaces as she lifted her skirts and hopped around in a mock can-can.

He wondered how long they would joke and chatter before they stirred themselves into leaving and wondered if he dared go over and tap on the window for Ellie's attention, but soon the lights were dimmed, and the door opened and the girls filed out squawking about the rain, their collars, and scarves, with feigned bad temper and noisy farewells. Ellie crossed the lane immediately and snuggled up to him in the doorway.

"Ah've known all t'time you were there, yer silly mug. Saw yer before, didn't ah when yer'd got yer head stuck in 'newspaper, that occupied yer couldn't catch sight o' me. Come on, luv."

She grabbed his arm and led him briskly through the Shambles towards the Vaults.

"Gor owt ter say, or is thi tongue tied?" she asked settling herself in a corner of a settle. "Mine's an egg flip, get what yer want, ah'm payin'. Useful 'aving a workin' lass, in't it?"

While Matt edged towards the counter to buy the drinks she opened her purse and attacked her face with rouge and lipstick.

"Not allowed it ovver theer. Soft in't it?" she called.

He watched her reflection in the glass behind the rows of fancy bottles. Her eggshell skin glowed luminously against the black timbered panelling, the curves of vermilion paint arched in brilliant contrast. There was a momentary glitter from the little gilt case which held her rouge and a flash of light from the mirror as she turned slightly to view herself. A wave of violet perfume drifted across the room jolted by the snap of her compact, followed by the zip of her purse and the slight smack of her lips as she compressed them together, released them, and settled her features into an expression of amused composure.

As Matt slipped onto the bench with the drinks she pulled off her headscarf and shook out her brown curls so that they brushed against her cheek. She toyed with the glass, twirling the stem and swilling its yellow contents around before she dipped her tongue delicately inside. Stealing a look across the bar to make sure that they were unobserved, she nuzzled her face forwards, pouting slightly, her eyes bright with humour.

"Ah wor tellin' 'em 'ow ah'd got a fancy man," she whispered, "That's what all t'laughing wor about."

She pressed her tongue between his lips and he tasted the residue of Advocaat as she explored with the tip, and felt her hand creep over his collar and her fingers engage in the hair on the nape of his neck.

"I shouldn't stay long," he said, loathe to tear himself away from the warmth of her body and the promise of even closer contact than last Saturday's encounter. "Got a lot of homework to get through, big trouble if I don't hand it in tomorrow morning, and there's hours of the damn stuff."

He gulped down his beer and made for the door.

"Come for me at tea-time before t'dance this week-end," Ellie asked, following, "if you don't think ah'm baby snatching."

She murmured the address and bus number in his ear before she gave him a shove in the behind.

"Don't worry luv, ah've telled mi mum ah'm bringin' a young man 'ome ter see er."

Matt ran off wondering what excuse he could give his mam this time; debating society, film club, play reading, what hadn't he used lately?

Chapter XXVI
LIKE MOTHER, LIKE DAUGHTER

Ellie's mother opened the door of the little terraced house and stood still for a moment looking at the fair-haired boy on the door step. Her hair was fixed in wave-grips and a net, and a cigarette dangled unlit from her mouth. She wore a rather coquettish frilly apron and pale blue furry slippers with clear plastic heels. Her hands were thrust into the pockets of a long knitted cardigan which was patterned with cockatoos in scarlet and navy blue, her shoulders hunched forward as if it were a colder day.

"Is Ellie in?" Matt began, "Is she back from work, yet?"

"No, she's not," the woman answered. She was tall, rather handsome, with good bones in her face and a long shapely neck circled with a string of pearls. She stepped back a pace and appraised him for a moment.

"But ah see she's got good taste. Yes ah allus said our Ellie knows what she's up to. Come in, lad, there's a nice fire in t'front room."

She led him down the passage and opened the door into a parlour that was inviting and warm, if a little overcrowded with knick-knacks in brass, flounced dolls and polka-dot net curtains.

"Get yerself comfy in 'ere luv, tek yer shoes off and mek yerself at 'ome, there's no ceremony 'ere. Ah'm glad yer've come early, ah'll 'ave somebody ter talk to while ah get ready, shan't ah?"

Soon she brought Matt a little tray with a cup of tea and a plate of chocolate marshmallows and set it on a pouffe next to an armchair. Taking hold of a lapel she guided him backwards across the room and playfully pushed him back into the chair, settling herself at his feet by the hearth.

He watched her take a coloured spill from a barbola vase on the mantelpiece, light it and transfer the flame to her cigarette. The Black Cat packet was empty. With a shrug she crumpled it and tossed it nonchalantly into the fire and watched it curl, burst alight, and then float upwards in charcoal shreds over the sparks. Tilting her head and inhaling she looked at him from the corner of her eyes. He smiled shyly and dropped his head. He noticed the silk slip she was wearing under the open cardigan and imperceptively followed its line as he sipped his tea, down to where it showed a lacy hem at the crook of her drawn-up knees.

She pulled a nail file, a small mirror and a pair of eyebrow tweezers from her pocket, eyeing him quizzically, and began her toilette.

"Don't mind me love, but there's a lot ter do ter get this lot straight afore ter'night. Talk about mutton dressed up as lamb."

She prodded him with the nail file.

"Come on lad, thar'll crack t'camera in a minute if thar not careful."

Her deep throated laugh shook her till she coughed, but she still retained the cigarette between her lips.

Matt shifted in his chair. "Ah'm not very good at chatting." he faltered. "What's yer name, I mean I didn't get Ellie's other name."

"Copestake, luv, but you can call me Lorna, ah don't like being Missus, not no more."

After a pause "What yer goin' ter be when yer leave school? Ellie tells me yer at t'Grammar."

Matt took a deep breath. "I'm going to be an actor, or a dancer if it's not too late."

She laughed uproariously. "Ooh, yer mean one o' them female impersonators. Bloody 'ell. Well, thar pretty enough."

The mirror and nail file clattered on to the hearth as she rose screaming to reveal the length of her legs, one knee crooked and turned in like a show-girl. Bending over the boy, she placed her hands on her hips and shook her breasts periously close to his teacup, then took off in a wild dance around the room, a parody of a low Music Hall turn. She strutted and minced, fluttering her eyelashes, slapped her thighs and stuck out her bottom with the silk slip pulled up to the waist and her painted nails curving the air as she danced.

Ellie was coming through the front door at that moment. She smiled hearing the rumpus going on, and dropped her bag on the frosted glass top of the hall table. When she entered the parlour she found her mother spreadeagled and exhausted in an abandoned finale pose across Matt's lap.

"Don't mind her, luv," she said, taking his teacup away, "She allus be'aves like a common tart. Thinks she's seventeen still. No need ter introduce yer then, ah see yer've already met."

"Seventeen, eh," Lorna retorted, posing in front of the mirror. "Not bad for an old bag, eh? Ah wish ah'd got my time all over again. Ah'd show you young uns a thing or two. There'd be no shilly shallying this time, cheeky."

Making for the door she turned suddenly.

"When thar done wi' 'er thar can 'ave a go at me." Winking she added "If thar a good lad."

Ellie turned on the radio and nibbled a marshmallow. They heard the splash of water in a tub out in the kitchen and Lorna singing as she prepared for a bath.

At Ellie's suggestion, Matt pushed the chairs back so that they could dance. It was Victor Sylvester music, more decorous than the boogie she favoured, but she syncopated with some incongruity against the strict tempo and wriggled against his body enough to arouse him. Teasingly she opened his collar and suggested he took off his jacket.

"Excuse me, ah'm not interrupting owt, am ah?"

Lorna burst into the room wearing a pair of french knickers and a brassiere. She began a frenzied search for a pair of stockings, looking in drawers, under cushions, in the Radio Times rack and under the sofa. She located them in the chrome fruit dish on the sideboard and threw them triumphantly over her shoulder, grabbed Matt away from Ellie and led him round the parlour in a close ballroom hold.

"Do yer come 'ere often?" she grinned, clucking him under the chin. "Yer stuck on our Ellie, aren't yer, poor lad, yer don't know what yer've got comin'."

Humming the tune from the radio, she strolled towards the door, trailing the stockings behind her. It was a credible imitation of Mae West grinding an exit with a silver fox stole.

She contrived a couple more appearances before and after her bath, once barely decently wrapped in a small towel, looking for a cigarette, and again later in fresh underwear, asking to borrow Ellie's flame nail varnish. Both times she managed a small suggestive contact with Matt; she brushed her fingers through his hair, squeezed his behind and looked knowingly across the room to her daughter.

Presently she left the pair and went upstairs to dress. It was Ellie's turn now in the bath. Matt lit a cigarette but choked and threw it in the fire. Lorna's voice came down the stairwell. "There's some gin in t'cabinet, luv. Pour yourself one, and one for me while yer at it."

When she entered, looking quite fashionably smart in padded shoulders, toque and wedges, expertly made up with puce lips lined in pencil, and silver eye-shadow delicately applied, Matt paused appreciatively before handing her the drink.

She perched on the arm of the sofa with her ankles crossed. "There's more coal ready in t'kitchen, duck, keep t'fire banked up and make yourselves warm, it's a chilly night. Nobody ull be disturbin' you."

She added an afterthought. "We don't see my feller, Ellie's dad, no more. 'E's pissed off rolling drunk round Lincolnshire, they can 'ave 'im."

Lorna stood, brushing a few flecks from her serge skirt, and handed Matt the empty glass. "It's nice 'aving a bloke around the 'ouse again, though," she winked. "Don't get up to anythin' ah wouldn't do."

Matt followed her into the passage and held the front door open for her. When he came back into the sitting room Ellie, dried and powdered was already lying waiting on the pegged rug.

Chapter XXVII

COME UNTO THESE YELLOW SANDS

A hot summer term drifted contentedly towards the long holiday. The french windows of the Upper School house remained permanently opened on to the lawns and the great lime trees under which boys snapped broken dried twigs as they sprawled, idly chatting and preparing their essays.

There was an alley between the vine-covered brick boundary walls and thick plantings of rhododendrons through which small groups wandered for a lecture from a master, and sometimes the housekeeper brought out trays of tea on to the stone-flagged terrace to sustain an alfresco tutorial.

It was Leonard Lomax, 'L.L.' to the boys, and Matt's adored housemaster, who had instituted these informal outdoor sessions which were soon copied by the other masters envious of the intimate and amusing relationship he so easily cultivated with his boys, but far too stiff in their attitudes to emulate his loose laconic style.

On a careless July afternoon as the shadows of the limes stirred across the scuffed central lawn and the late lupins and foxgloves cracked their pods in the dry borders, 'L.L.' arranged his slight dandified frame into an arc, leaning elegantly against a raised urn of blazing magenta geraniums. He held his cup and saucer apart, the little finger of his right hand crooked away from the handle, and coughed discreetly, the ash from the Gold Flake in his mouth falling in a slow cascade down the front of his black silk gown.

"You should have seen them, dears," he croaked, and after a few more rasping little coughs, "Robertson and Hare, master farceurs, darlings of the West End. Could get more laughs out of a simple thing like a cup of tea than most actors get in a lifetime. A question of technique, yer see, practice." He pursed his downward tilting lips and huffed through his cigarette until it glowed again.

The shirt-sleeved boys lay smiling on the wide steps beneath the terrace where he posed. They were used to these non-sequiturs. 'L.L.', during the last half-hour had drifted amiably from the untimely death of the young Rimbaud to the exquisite textural torture of Van Gogh's paint, through the revolutionary and galvanising effect of Gorden Craig on the design and lighting of twentieth century theatre, Craig's betrayal of Isadora Duncan, on to the influence of Delius in English music, and a breakdown of the excerpts he, 'L.L.' had taken from the available Delius recordings to underlay his forthcoming production for a local amateur theatre group of Shaw's St. Joan.

Medically exempted from the services, the war had obliged him to leave a successful peacetime career as an actor and theatre director and he had found in this Midlands town a refuge where he could still satisfyingly, if only in a limited way, follow his vocation.

"Which brings me to the point," he said, fixing his gaze on Matt and dabbing at his mouth with a silk handkerchief as he set down the cup and saucer on the stone balustrade.

"By the way, did you see my adams apple move at all while I took my tea?"

"What's that got to do with the price of sliced bread?" the boy queried.

"As I was saying, Bedford. By the way, did you ever see 'Rookery Nook?' Anyone? No? What an uncultivated load of heathens."

And after a pause, "I was glorious, simply glorious in that once, a very long time ago. Didn't know the words, went on in a hurry for an actor who was sick, or was he drunk . . . I expect, yes, he was drunk, lousy bum of a player, old school, useless. I wrote the whole damn stuff out on little cards and placed it about the set, you know, by the phone, in the drawers, in the bookcase, etc, etc, then got the whole blasted thing mixed up. Did Act Three first, then back to Act One, kept picking up the wrong bleeding card. You'd think I'd get one right by chance, but no, and a top agent was out front, dear oh dear."

"Bedford," he murmured, "You, yes you, beautiful little heathen with those," he paused for an appreciative titter from the class, "those scandalously intoxicating grey eyes, your come-uppance has arrived. As you have seduced me, so you shall seduce the world. You shall play Ariel. Next term. Get a copy from the Bursar, read the text. You will be word perfect for the first rehearsal, no time for mugging. Smile, boy, you'll be perfect for the part." His eyes burned through the thick pebble glasses as he pursed his lips and blew a kiss to the young actor.

The warmth of the afternoon, locked into the rambling garden, had seeped into the boys' bones. They yawned and stretched, smiling fondly at the eccentric tutor who had goaded their brains towards the opening of the maze of sensibility he longed for them to enter.

"Bedford, you look dumbstruck, or are you trying to suppress a fart?"

"I expect he's overcome at the prospect of playing a fairy," proffered Matt's chum Keith, nudging him.

They all turned to look at Matt who was sitting now cross-legged, his chin on his chest, his cheeks burning.

He slowly raised his head, gratefully aware of the support and warmth of his peer group.

"I only hope I'm up to it, Lenny, but thanks."

"Hare-brained saucepot," 'L.L.' yelled, coughing away his cigarette.

"God, you boys, do I need a cudgel to get through to you?. This is your world, you can make it or break it, knead it, mould it, eat it or spit it out. You can be dreary, dull, lifeless, or God willing, entertaining, amusing, outstanding . . . . like me." He winked. "See you soon," he grinned, ambling towards the high gates set in the crumbling wall.

Turning, he clutched his tattered gown around his crumpled suit. "Diaghilev, look him up by the way, Ballet Russes, Nijinsky, Benois, Karsarvina, etc, said to Stravinsky, or was it his second amour, Lifar . . . . . Etonne moi! . . . . . Astonish me."

Then directly to Matt, "I'll be looking to you for a bit of the same, cock. Do you read me, boy. Ta rah."

Matt read and re-read *The Tempest* throughout the holidays. He was used to unravelling scripts as he had already played many parts for the School which had a centuries old tradition of playing Shakespeare, and there were also a considerable number of local amateur theatre companies who had found Matt to be a useful and keen junior player.

The role of Ariel presented him with many challenges. The songs were set in a high treble, and with his voice overdue for breaking he had to take care not to overtax it.

"Sing down an octave," the lady pianist hissed at rehearsals, "We don't want the baby to run away with the bath water."

"Dance on now," 'L.L.' yelled.

"I don't know how," Matt shouted from the wings.

"Well bloody well find out, you arsehole," came the reply from the back of the theatre. "Make it up . . . . . do something . . . . . at least have something you can change later."

'L.L.' took him out to tea after the rehearsal.

"Look here, nature boy, this should be right up your street. It's no good you careening up and down those blasted colliery tips in that godforsaken village of yours and swanning about the moors like some pantheistic young hooligan if you can't translate all that nature worship rubbish into something I can use in this damn play. Look . . . I don't want you to give me arabesques and pointed feet as if you were a blasted ballet dancer. You're playing a primitive . Get into the bones of this wild creature. He's born of the winds and sunlight and spells. He wasn't trained by Ninette fucking de Valois. Get on with it, Ariel is a flash of lightning, a thunderclap, an electric storm . . . . . Oh God, this is driving me up the wall . . . . . Waitress, another plate of cakes for the young Olivier please."

'L.L.' had indeed prepared a beautiful and original production. The stage was lined on three sides and overhead with silvery grey parachute silk, salvaged from an abandoned air base by an enterprising stage manager, on to which were cast the giant shadows of leaves and grasses hung in front of the lanterns in the wings. The silk was billowed from behind, especially in the storm sequence, and every entrance of Ariel was marked by a fall of glitter dust from the flies.

"Stand still," the make-up lady pleaded at the dress rehearsal. "How can I get this slap on with you wriggling about like an eel?" The goosefleshed boy was standing on a table in a side room dressed in a baggy pair of borrowed swim trunks.

"These'll have to come off or I won't be able to get the wet-white in all the right places, and you'll show bare flesh when you put your jock strap on." When Matt blushingly demurred she yanked the trunks down over his thighs and slapped the cold sponge over his bare buttocks.

"No time for modesty here, lovey," she said, "I've pulled out more than you've got with a pin from a winkle. But anyway, I'll let you do your own front, I don't want you getting excited."

The almost non-existent costume consisted of the briefest cod-piece constructed from a few acorns and leaves sprayed with silver paint and a matching chaplet worn over his similarly sprayed hair. His eyelids and lips were painted green and he was given plaited cellophane bracelets to wear on his wrists and ankles.

His teeth chattered as he tried going through his lines for the last time while the final touches were made and the cast assembled for the final dress parade.

"Gawd," said 'L.L.', when he got down the line to Matt, slapping him on the rear, "You look like the fucking fairy on the Christmas tree. OK everyone, beginners please, all on stage and good luck."

The performances of the play were a wonder to the boy. Gongs and bells crashed and tinkled every time he careered on to the stage, and a harpist in the wings playing glissandi covered his exits. He found that he could pause, crouched in a spotlight, and fix a stare into the dark void of the auditorium for much longer than he had thought possible in rehearsal, then breathe, spring up, turn and stare again before delivering his next line. He felt a power in his limbs, standing akimbo in the footlights, tilting his head to catch the light from the follow spot before he fell prostrate at the feet of Prospero, his master magician. The songs were delicately set and unearthly. He poised on half-toe and sang with strong clear voice that rang commandingly through the theatre, surprising himself with the clarity and conviction he could summon up.

His dancing was his own untrained and utterly natural version of his observation of the flight of birds and the scuttering of wild animals, unhindered by the constraints of formal training other than having learned in the gymnasium and on the track-field how to tumble and somersault like an athlete.

After the performances he would sit on the top deck of the bus taking him home hugging to himself the memory of the night's excitements and the deep satisfaction of having faced and won an audience. Wedged into his seat between familiar earthbound figures he closed his eyes and soared in fantastic parabolas, his back arched like a bow ready to unleash an arrow, curving effortlessly through an endless space in a revolving spiral of soft bounds and leaps. He was in communion with the ancient Lords of the Dance and he had already begun the first ritual.

The following weeks were depressing for Matt. He was behind with his school work, having spent so much time in rehearsal and performance. The back-log of translation, reading and essay writing was an unbearable chore, and of course he could not pay proper attention to the current work in progress.

There were other major distractions. Ballet Rambert came to the town, performing in a factory canteen as part of a C.E.M.A. tour. Ravishing and amusing as the performance of the brilliant little company were, with the lithe young John Gilpin, Belinda Wright and the remarkable repertoire of Tudor, Gore, Ashton and Howard, Matt's initial euphoria quickly drained away as he began to realise he would never dance professionally like these finely tuned bodies unless he began training.

The Rambert were followed by the lavish company of Mona Inglesby, International Ballet, playing at the Sheffield Lyceum and the world famous Ballet Jooss with their remarkable allegory of war, 'The Green Table'.

Matt watched all the performances from the gallery on begged and borrowed money, played truant from school to sneak into the theatre during the daytime to watch classes and rehearsals, and at home, late into the night, bent and stretched his body in front of the sideboard mirror into the shapes he had seen the dancers make.

There was a single dancing school in the town. One Saturday afternoon he steeled himself for the general class, presenting himself in vest and shorts, barefoot, at the barre.

He was horrified at the ensuing parody of dance training. Fat little girls flung themselves without warm-up into grotesque backbends, flick-flacks and overs, while a dozen others tackled an energetic tap routine. The peroxided teacher played the piano, chainsmoking, gossiping with a collection of mothers, without ever turning to watch her pupils. She sauntered over to Matt and eyed him up and down.

"Hm," she breathed, "not bad shape. Could do with a bit of male talent round here. Can you do the splits?"

She yanked one of his legs into the air and pushed his foot up higher than his head.

"Yer, you'll do. Just join in love and follow from behind."

Matt realised instinctively that anything he learned from Mavis Earnshaw would very quickly have to be unlearned. After his one and only session with her he stuck to the Latin American class with the Convent girls and the jiving with Ellie.

It was late on a Tuesday evening when Ma Bedford barred and bolted the shop door. Normally she would have paused to catch a breath of air and admire the softly-lit windows of the houses across the field where coal fires and gas brackets glimmered faintly through curtains of net and brocade, or to wave to a late homecomer hurrying down the lane.

But she was feeling unusually fatigued and irritable and kicked aside the doormat which had been propped against the door to hold it ajar, muttering to herself in aggravation at the litter of sweet wrappers, cigarette ends and leaves swirling in a little eddy down the passage.

"Ah'm that browned off," she said glumly, ramming home the bolt, "ah feel 'emmed in an' cut off like a goldfish swimmin' round on its own in a bowl."

She cocked her head listening to Jess pottering about getting the tea ready in ι kitchen and began again with louder intonation when she knew she held him audience.

"There's times when ah feel penned in like an animal in a cage at t'bloody zoo, like yer see at bloody Belle Vue, t'only difference is folk pay ter see curiosities like them an' ah'm a free peepshow standin' 'ere all day bendin', stretchin' and servin' ungrateful buggers what thinks yer their slave from mornin' till night."

The Wednesday ritual was unchangeable. She loved her outing into the town to scour the market, have her hair done, meet Matt for tea and take him to the pictures. Sometimes for a rare treat they ran for the Sheffield bus and spent an excited hour in the big stores and then saw a show in one of the grand theatres, coming home late on the slow train.

"It won't be same without yer duck tomorrow," she said, ruffling Matt's hair as she flopped down at the kitchen table.

"Ah think ah wain't go to Sheffield on mi own, as yer waint be coming, ah don't like sittin' on t'bus seein' all that bomb damage. By 'eck it took a thumpin', din't it . . . . Anyroad, where was it yer said yer goin' tomorrow, duck?"

"To London," Matt said. "I've got to go for this audition. I've worked out the train times. I'll be back about eleven o'clock."

"Ah wish it could 'ave bin another day," his mother said in a low voice, "though ah suppose ah've got to get used to t'idea mi own little lad's grown up an' is goin' to leave 'ome an' leave 'is mam what loves 'im."

They ate the meal in silence while outside in the dark children whooped around the gennils. Jess stole a few proud furtive looks at the boy, remembering how when he was a shafer, Matt had vaulted gates and ditches like a kid goat and had run like the wind to be swept up in his arms as he stepped off the gantry from the pit cage.

Matt watched his mother wash her face at the stone sink in the corner. She dried herself slowly and pulled a comb through her thick dark waves.

"It's a mystery to me," she said, eyeing Matt through the small oval mirror, "why can't you stop 'ere with yer own folk what love you and would do anything for you."

"With all respect, mother," the boy said, hating the cold-seeming indifference in his voice, "this is something you can't help me with, other than at least tell me that for my sake you're willing to let me go."

When his mother and father had gone to bed the boy stayed up late listening to the radio with the sound turned down low, twiddling with the knobs for foreign stations.

Up in the front bedroom his mother lay awake, listening to the faint crackling of the wireless and the distant creak and grinding of the colliery machinery. She wondered if birds or animals felt the same kind of pain when fledglings left the nest or young foxes went to fend for themselves. The vast old bedstead and the thick creamy eiderdown cocooned her into sleep as the siren for the night shift moaned along the embankment and a slow goods train wound its way through the cutting.

Chapter XXVIII

HOME AND AWAY

When May left school a distant relative of her father arranged a job for her in a garden nursery on the other side of town. The outside work in all weathers suited her. She was lithe and athletic, capable of keeping up with many of the older girls and youths there, and the work was deeply satisfying to her nature. Many of the tasks for the juniors were repetetive and needed painstaking attention. They laboured along the precise rows of saplings with stiff fingers on icy mornings before the mist had cleared from the fields, and if the rain fell heavily, spent long hours in the glasshouses planting endless boxes of seedlings, cuttings and tubers. She felt at peace with the closely-ordered work, her hands plunged into moist sand and peat deftly moving in swift patterns through the beds.

The nurture of these exquisite little plants brought rich rewards. First, leaves uncurling, minute flower buds swelling, then the gradual growth of stems until there were great banks of brilliant colour. As the days of summer lengthened the men tied in the new tendrils of vine and clematis overhead and the sunlight filtered through the green bower making irregular patterns of light and shade over the benches.

While May's hands were busy planting, weeding, propagating, part of her mind was elsewhere. She still mourned for Reg; the image of the bridal bouquet which Freda had placed lovingly on his grave had seared an indelible impression, and she grieved for her mother who had been irrevocably hurt. The boys were growing up and increasingly occupied with their own pastimes, sometimes guilty for escaping from the sorrowing household.

The evenings in the Barlows' kitchen were oppressive. There were long silences, whole hours of acute unspoken misery which seemed almost to materialise into a solid and tangible presence. Her father, always a man of few words and little natural good humour, retreated further into himself and was no comfort to his wife.

He was helpless when sometimes she got up from her chair and went to unlatch the door, scanning the field, looking for Reg coming home whistling. It was cruel that the habit had not died with her son and he could not bear to see the anguish in her eyes when the jarring reality struck. It was May who went to put an arm round her mother's shoulder and lead her gently down the yard. They walked to the bottom of the row and across the rough grass to the embankment railing and watched the sun hover low over the sloping fields beyond.

The blow to her family brought May to the end of her childhood. In the months that followed, contented in her work and faced with the responsibility of carrying her parents through their mourning, she crossed the threshold early and became a young woman.

"She's a saint, that girl," declared Ma Bedford. "There's not many young lasses who'd look after their mam like what she does. Most on 'em 'ould be gaddin' about, dancin', pictures, at 'er age, but she's a trojan, mark my words."

Matt listened and marked her words, although he was already convinced. They were growing apart though, he thought. He saw a lot less of her now that she was working and he was becoming increasingly occupied with events after school hours and at weekends.

"Haven't seen much of you lately," May said one evening when they came back to the village on the same bus. "But then, we've both been busy."

"Yes," he replied defensively. "I've had a lot of extra work to do and a lot of nights are taken up with societies and things. I'm in a play soon. Will you come?"

"Oh, I expect you've had plenty on, enough to stop you from fetching me like you used to," she answered.

She looked out of the window at the traffic swishing by in the half light of the autumn evening. Yellow headlights pierced the steamed up windows. With the cuff of her duffle jacket she wiped a clean circle in the glass and peered out. "Who's the little number, then?" Matt held his breath. "Ah don't mind, you're your own master, just thought ah'd ask, that's all."

"Who do you mean May, what little number?" His voice was low and expressionless.

"O come on, Mr. Innocent, you know very well who she is when you're with her." After a moment she turned and looked him full in the face. "There used to be a time when we told each other everything. At least I did. Maybe you weren't so forthcoming." The bus lurched and juddered up the steep last hill towards the village. He was glad of the few moments it took for the other passengers and themselves to dismount.

They stood at the end of the lane for a while without saying anything. Matt looking down at his satchel which he had put at his feet. "Not much to tell," he mumbled. "There's this girl I met I've seen a few times, we've been out dancing, nothing special."

May turned and began walking the lane and he followed miserably. "Spreading your wings, lad, that's what it's called," she said softly over her shoulder. "I had 'er pointed out to me in t'Picture queue other day. Ellie, that's what she's called, i'nt it? Ne'er mind, duck, you're welcome if that's what yer after. And if she's giving you what yer want."

They had reached the top of May's row. He came towards her and saw the tears in her eyes.

"You're wrong, May. She isn't giving me anything at all."

The lie stood between them for a long time. May wondered why she did not yet want to give him her body, since in her mind it was pledged long ago, and Matt knew that he had fallen in love.

He was a guileless boy so it took a while for him to learn how to avoid Ellie or any of her invitations without offence. He was anxious also not to cross Mrs. Copestake, who managed to swoop on him in quite unexpected places, full of winking umbrage that he had not visited the little house recently. Ma Bedford conveyed several messages from Ellie after eating alone in the tea room, Matt always having found a good excuse not to join her there.

She was intrigued by the vivacious girl who attended to her so nicely and saved special cakes behind the counter on Wednesdays. "That lass in Woodheads wor askin' about you," she would say. "Ah thought you didn't know 'er when we wor in there that time? Or 'ave you come across 'er since?" Fortunately for Matt many of his mother's questions did not require an answer, especially if she was engrossed over her account books or counting the ration coupons. But in this case he had one ready to foist off any further questioning if she warmed to her subject. He told his mother firmly that he hardly knew the girl. She had a cousin at his school and he had met her once at somebody's birthday party. This seemed to allay a certain apprehension. Ma Bedford smiled at her son.

"Ah'm glad, duck. She's a nice kid but ah bet she can be as fauce as a brass monkey, that minx, she's a bit forward."

There was a hint of anxiety when his father took him for a walk a couple of days later. The ominous command "Get thy coat lad, ah want thee ter come for a walk wi' me," invariably heralded a dressing down for some misdemeanour, or worse, as happened now, a stumbling embarrassed homily into morals and bodily functions.

Jess Bedford tried hard but failed. If he was curious to know whether his son had already sinned, or indeed knew how to break the commandment, his efforts were in vain. Matt maintained a slightly baffled but interested expression throughout the interview. He shook his head or nodded when required as they strolled self-consciously, and afterwards politely thanked his father for the trouble he was taking. And Jess happily reported back to Ma Bedford that the lad had kept himself to himself.

In the last summer holiday of his time at school, Matt spent most of his days looking forward to the hour when he met May after her work. Sometimes they took a bus to Youlgreave, Lathkil Dale, or Tideswell, and spent the long evening wandering. Or there were concerts in the City Hall with Ferrier, Baillie or Titterton. The Wolfit Company and the Carl Rosa Opera did seasons in the nearby towns, and they had the whole of Sundays to visit Haddon, Chatsworth, Hardwick and Newstead Abbey. They knew that a part of their lives was coming to an end and they filled their heads with sights and sounds that they could remember when they were apart.

At the bottom of a trunk he put a battered atlas and three volumes of pressed specimens, English flowers, weeds, grasses, painstakingly mounted and identified. There followed an album of family snap-shots, a giant photograph of the School Group 1947 and the cured pelt of a white rabbit. From a considerable pile of loose-leaved folders which contained the past year's output he chose some favourite work, not sure whether he wanted to keep it for future reference or merely as a sentimental keepsake of his school days. He had been in a panic suddenly, struck with the finality of leaving his studies and his friends who were preparing for the Universities. He wondered if he would forget everything he had learned, away from academic disciplines, and leafed many times through the collection of essays in the dog-eared manilla folders. They represented in tangible form the sum of his present knowledge. But it was impracticable to take everything. The choice having been made he burned the rest.

Some weeks later Matt was installed in a flat with a couple of other students. It was the top floor of a decaying Victorian terraced house in Colville Square near the Portobello Road and Notting Hill Gate. He had fixed photographs and theatre programmes on the walls of his room to disguise the fading wallpaper as best he could, and in front of the iron grate he had placed a cracked vase full of mauve irises stolen from the Square Garden. He wrote May the following letter:-

Dear May,

I expect, or should I say hope, that you're wondering about me, and what's become of me. I'll start that again. I'm desperate to know if you think about me at all, sometimes, mostly, or all of the time. You won't believe me but I think about you all the time. No that's a lie. The days are long and very hard. I crawl back here at the end of the day and climb the stairs on my knees. Then I think about you. Is that enough? Let me know. Here is a little room a bit like the attic in Boheme, though not nearly as big, just as scruffy. I have a window and a tiny balcony. I can sit out on the window sill five floors up and I'm almost in a lime tree. Down below there's a garden. Not what you would call a garden, more a bed of pebbles, very dusty. There is a thrush that comes and sings to me in my tree and I've taken to pinching flowers to cheer up my room. I've got a large vase of Chinese looking irises at the moment. Last week I had a great branch of almond blossom strung up in the ceiling. When it died it fell like confetti all over the carpet. I have a friend who's mad about Ferrier. She brings a record player up here or I climb over the roof because she lives next door in the attic (no it's not like that, she's a dedicated ballet student, only eats yoghourt), and we play Ferrier while it gets dark in the Square below. The lamps go swaying down the road, you can see for miles. I think about you and everyone at home, not in the same way of course. Can you believe I'm happy? But there's a great deal I'm missing, mostly you and the folks. Give them my love. I'm sending you this book of poems by D. H. Lawrence, I found in a bookshop near here. I hope you enjoy it. Look especially at page fourteen, the top of the page I've marked in pencil.

Miss you,
MATT

The marked passage was the opening stanza of *End of another home holiday,* and ran as follows:-

When shall I see the half-moon sink again
Behind the black sycamore at the end of the garden?
When will the scent of the dim white phlox
Creep up the wall to me, and in my open window?